The Secret Crypt

Salvador Elizondo

THE SECRET CRYPT

Translated from the Spanish by Joshua Pollock

DALKEY ARCHIVE PRESS
Dallas / Dublin

Originally published in Spanish by Joaquín Mortiz as *El hipogeo secreto* in 1968.

Library of Congress Cataloging-in-Publication Data
Names: Elizondo, Salvador, 1932-2006, author. | Pollock, Joshua, trans-lator.
Title: The secret crypt / Salvador Elizondo ; translated by Joshua Pollock.
Other titles: Hipogeo secreto. English
Description: First Dalkey Archive edition. | McLean, IL : Dalkey Archive Press, 2018.
Identifiers: LCCN 2022933515 | ISBN 9781628974386 (pbk. : acid-free paper)
Classification: LCC PQ7298.15.L5 H513 2018 | DDC 863/.64--dc23
LC record available at https://lccn.loc.gov/2022933515

www.dalkeyarchive.com
Dallas / Dublin

Printed on permanent/durable acid-free paper.

For María

Introduction
Joshua Pollock

"All writing is the attempt to comprehend and convey a vision that is maybe or perhaps incomprehensible, maybe or perhaps incommunicable."

Salvador Elizondo

ON ITS SURFACE, Salvador Elizondo's 1968 antinovel *The Secret Crypt* is about a writer named Salvador Elizondo writing a novel called *The Secret Crypt*. The characters in his novel know they are being written, and plot to overthrow the writer and seize control of their destiny. The ontological layers of this pseudo-plot nest inside of, and then begin to spill into, one another. The book centers on a secret society, a ruined city, plans for a sacrificial killing—a lost arctic explorer even blunders through—but anybody reading *The Secret Crypt* for plot will be disappointed. The book is a purely linguistic experiment. César Aira, in his *Diccionario de Autores Latinoamericanos*, referred to it as a text "comprised entirely of self-reference." Elizondo states as much when he opens the second section of the book with a statement of his poetics: "Writing a book is, in a sense, rereading. The text builds itself out of its own repeated reading." In this way, *The Secret Crypt* constructs itself out of its own hermetic substance, and the reader assembles the text in his or her complicit reception of it. This act of writing through rereading is reminiscent of translation.

The Secret Crypt is an attempt to unravel what happens in the act of writing. It is a space of sheer literary creation—everything within it refers back to the fundamental translation from thought to word. Elizondo's language, its wild beauty and moldy baroqueness, performs feats of creation and collapse. As he constructs his ideal cities in language his sentences get carried away with themselves, breathless, hyperbolic, until they buckle under their own weight and topple into near-incomprehensibility. This collapse, the undoing of meaning, or at least the calling-into-question of communication, is at the heart of *The Secret Crypt*. Unlike those bourgeois novels (read in "those houses . . . which have beautiful fruit bowls"), Elizondo is not interested in searching for lost time or narrating a story; his game is to undo the world, to disturb our sense of ourselves, and return us to some primordial oblivion at the origin of language ("the fuzzy figuration of a world of pure causality . . .").

Always troubled by the limits of language, I found myself mainly interested in the book as a text that plays with various types of translations—from thought to word, image to language, as transmission from one mind to another, as invocation, as codebreaking, as traitor, imposter, usurper, as subverter of univocality—a text that assumes the form of one thing to pass off another. Each author in the book is, like the translator, constrained by the bounds of another, more primary, author's text, all of it but an attempt at writing beyond "that supreme fallacy that is reality." I was also compelled by the sense that Elizondo was grappling with the idea that there is something authoritarian about authorship, a desire for order and control he wanted to subvert with his decadent and failed tale of a bumbling brotherhood trying to seize power.

The Secret Crypt presents a difficult task for its translator. In the process I've had moments of feeling vinyl-bound (with a ball gag), moments of feeling like a sleep-deprived conspirator, and of performing a macabre parody of the author—a trancelike ritual not unlike the one portrayed in Jean Rouch's film *The Mad Masters*. In the end, I approached the text as one most often does, word by word, sentence by sentence, page by page, trying to recreate Elizondo's purple prose, his dazzling explosions and stilted dead-ends, his paradoxes and philosophical jaunts. If there are passages where language seemingly loses its communicative faculty and obscures any possible meaning, if there are places where Elizondo's prose seems to come unmoored from the world of concrete concepts, this is all a part of the novel's texture: it is the struggle of creation, in which Elizondo makes the reader participate. I have let the text guide me, staying true to what I believe Elizondo intended. Of course, it is not my job to clean up the messy aspects of the book (nor to apologize for his sexism), but the text also soars in places, and it is my job to do justice to that. I can only hope that to some extent I have. Sadly, with the author having passed away, and thus having transcended (or perhaps become entombed in) language, his translators can only follow the trail Elizondo left when he wrote, "Where does the real person hide? Perhaps behind these words, like the fly peeking out from the translucency of amber."

This translation is the result of six years of fits and starts. I first became interested in Elizondo after reading his earlier novel *Farabeuf*. I had heard Elizondo referred to as the Mexican Robbe-Grillet—which was enough to pique my interest—and I appreciated the way he broke free from the dominant trends of boom-era Latin American literature. I believe he was doing something unique in the space of 1960s Mexico: his early novels make almost no reference to the national tropes of his peers; he eschews any trace of realism (magical or otherwise); and his transgressive vision (which has more to do with Bataille and de Sade than the politics of his moment) was beyond taboo for his context. When I read *El Hipogeo Secreto*—my version of which became *The Secret Crypt*—I decided I was up for a challenge and began to translate it. I wanted to lose myself in language. Over the years the project stalled a number of times, owing largely to a bureaucratic misunderstanding about who held the rights and my own unstable life, but it never quite died. This final version has been improved many times by the editorial suggestions of (first) Jeremy Davies and (more recently) Eric Kurtzke, Jake Snyder, and Alistair

Ian Blyth. I would also like to thank Paulina Lavista for her blessings and permission. After a long and labyrinthine relationship with it, I will be relieved finally to submit, three times in a row, to the forgetting of this accursed book.

The Secret Crypt

But the world, mind, is, was and will be writing its own
wrunes for ever, man, on all matters that fall under the ban
of our infrarational senses . . .

                – James Joyce, *Finnegans Wake*

". . . TELL ME, I IMPLORE YOU," he says, "the night would have been forgotten, lost to the darkest oblivion. Evoke, evoke the dream which must be realized, here, now. We have only a few moments. Let's try to figure out how you participated in the events. Everything, like a slow-motion dance. It's all there: a source; the mouth in which the dream becomes word. Pray; that your words invoke the guides. Our discipline is like a plain that we'll cross at a gallop, a cart pulled by the horses of crime. Please; I implore you. Try to concentrate. Three times in a row remember and forget that luminous wound. Set aside your own desires and surrender yourself to the plan . . . The word . . . Take me . . . Break me, I am but a weak reed in your fist . . . That's it; repeat after me: 'Break me . . . Pluck off my petals as if I were the Fire Flower . . . the blood that burns, that spills

across the edges of the wound from which it flows . . .'
Descend like death's own vultures into vast ravines and
remember; remember and forget three times in a row the
words written in this book; remember and exhaust the
words contained on this page: coins between your sharp
fingertips; sand, a memento of desolate mountains dropped
into your frozen lap; sand stuck to the anxious skin of your
thighs. Motionless. That's it. Don't move. This is an
extremely important part of our discipline. Now forget.
Forget it all. Drive those drunken horses out of sight. Don't
think about the night, now. Everything is dawn, the first
cracks are beginning to appear; marble columns collapsing
in the peristyles of your memory. We have to attempt it this
very evening. Remember and forget it three times, until the
memory crumbles to dust once more, mere ash to be scattered by time, say the members of Urkreis, as they make
another attempt to complete the experiment. It's crucial that
you shatter to pieces, this very evening, Perra. As you submit
to that great discipline, that madness, that forgetting of your
name through which you will be purified, I will move
toward the dawn of your memory, will cross the night to
drink at your source, at the source of your name I'll evoke
our first encounter, and our second, and our third, and then
I'll forget the third and I'll forget the second and—as morning approaches—I'll keep the first beside my heart; and then
another obliteration of your name and the memory of your
name, of your costume and the memory of your expression,
of your eyes and the memory of your name, of your costume
and of your wounds, and of those disturbing scenes, your
little victories in the darkness of a museum of frozen words,

of the myth and the word and the word that is myth and
the ceremony of that apparition in a passageway furrowed
like the raging waters of a river or sea: mirrors in which the
dance of the Fire Flower subsides and equations crack like
the shafts of the columns of the deserted peristyles where
we, the members of Urkreis, first dreamed of initiating you
into the most immense of all terrors: that of forgetting your
name and even the memory of your name, Perra. Come,
Perra, come. But don't move. This is important. Just show
yourself and repeat these words: 'Break me, I am but a weak
reed in your fist, I am but a filthy word on your lips, I am
but a flower of fire, a dog too stupid to sit still in a dark
room; defoliate me with your gasping breath, as if I were
the Fire Flower; crop my ears and tail and teach me to forget
myself because I am a dog; teach me to submerge myself in
the oblivion of those ill-fated nights in depraved theaters,
in the accursed flickering of footlights, under the eyes of the
Know-it-all, there, in the orchestra, sitting with his back to
the stage, open to the surgical stare of a few spectators . . .'
Yes, repeat after me; now repeat the memory of your name:
'Mía, Mía,' a sketchy character at best, but still the most
prominent, in a book written in a code whose key has been
lost and whose decryption now relies on ambiguous data,
on unreliable research, on false impressions, on a secret
chronicle that is, to an extent we cannot trace with any precision, precisely the heritage upon which our lives have been
founded; that is the nucleus around which we develop those
activities that inspire our modest circle of philosophical
scholars. You don't blame us, I hope? You aspired to this
submission. You went missing, disappearing into our arms,

into all of our mouths, into the mirrors of our eyes, where
you perhaps discovered your true appearance, and where
someone—perhaps the Pantokrator Himself—called you by
your true name, there beneath an enormous arch; it was
either somebody you happened to bump into, turning a
corner, or someone with whom we'd set up a meeting, to
discuss literary matters, beneath an enormous tree, after the
rain; maybe it was even the Pantokrator Himself who called
you by your true name under a vast, sunny portico, that pale
monument, which the natives or else those who migrated
here erected to honor the shade, and you saw yourself
reflected in that name as if in a mirror, and you opened your
legs that the moonlight might enter your body as a rat enters
the contorted mouth of a cadaver, as a rat takes refuge in
the heat of a woman's sex as she sleeps among the rubble of
a wall demolished by the winds of millennia. You would
have been able to dictate it to us then, this book that we're
vainly attempting to write—all of it, after ten thousand
generations of fools assembling letters and symbols to learn
His true name, the name of Pantokrator. But we knew that
you knew it; we looked into your eyes and were sure. The
mark of your name was visible on your body, like a cancer,
like an allusion to the mythical salamander, like a scorpion;
igneous vermin burning in your chest; demented words,
whose utterance would have given us command of every
city, of the secret of all architecture. How tall you would
have been. And now there's barely time. With your eyes,
you cried out to be subjected to our discipline, you roamed
among the fractured colonnades, in whose shade we occasionally sought refuge, so as to pass, in secret, close to that

identity already known to you. You already know the secret
that we were trying to discover by observing the shadow cast
by the gnomon of the obelisk as it moves across the agora.
But in exchange for a drink of water you would have told
us a little something about it, in those burning summer
days. And then the beggars and invalids, the pariahs that
inhabit that ruined city, told us that you slept leaning
against the empty doorways, and that when you slept, your
body dreamed of endless self-torture, of fornication and
numbers, because your lips formed those words and rattled
off never-ending ciphers. H saw you sleeping at dawn, lying
down in a plaza without a statue, and sensed that your body
was filled with gold, noting down all the numbers that
issued from your mouth. The next day he told us everything, but his description placed too much emphasis on the
roundness of your breasts, the length of your legs. He formulated a vague hypothesis as to your speech, which made
us laugh to ourselves (we, who are beyond the bounds of
laughter): namely that in your sleep you were uttering the
entire sequence of prime numbers, out to figures incredibly
remote. So greatly did we laugh at H that he began to confuse things all the more, his description of your ardor and
his own speculations thereon becoming mixed up with
imprecise theorems about the relationship between certain
characteristics of the figure of the quadratrix and the deter-
mination of this series' terms. The editors of the *Jahrbuch
über die Fortschritte der Mathematik* politely rejected his
work, though not without a certain note of sarcasm. But in
secret all of us went out to watch you sleep. At night, our
faces covered like bandits (yes, like conspirators too), we

would go to the great fractal staircases, overrun with grass,
or to the demolished shrines, to watch you dream your
dreams. It's clear, isn't it, that all of this is a lie? Who would
have been able to testify to your oracular, arithmetical condition if, at the end of that summer, we had already known
that it was us you were dreaming? None of the adherents of
our society would ever have dared wake you in the middle
of the night to fulfill your dream of slow coitus, fearful lest
it bring about our deaths. By the time the grass growing in
the cracks in the stones began to wither and the wind
snatched at its golden blades in the cold angles of the ruins,
we were already subject to the insurmountable terror pro-
duced by your dream, that magnificent city of which we
ourselves were the inhabitants. Perhaps, if at some point you
woke, the walls would fall, a sea of wakefulness would
undermine the implacable foundation of that dream inside
which we dwelled, dedicated—foolish as we were—to a
collection of erroneous, of infinitely mistaken hypotheses
about the identity that (perhaps tonight) will be revealed to
us. A shudder runs through the hand with which I write
this report—the letters that establish our ritual freeze like
insects imprisoned in the enthusiasm of their flight, in the
amber which, now melting, allows them suddenly to move
once more—as I remember that night when I watched you
as you slept and, myself wide open, like a door flung wide
onto a panorama of stars, drunk on the night and held fast
like a fly in the amber of your dream, I foresaw the delirious
ceremony of your awakening. A desolation vaster than the
ruined landscape's reigned in my senses, and you were like
a recumbent statue beginning to peek out from your hiding

place. I was thirsty to learn of the origins of my night; I wanted to know the exact disposition of this prison in which I was locked. I reveled in the knowledge you contemplated, knowledge I imagined myself able to acquire. I saw you from some chink in stonework as coarse as the concretion of a natural, organic fact. The barely perceptible rhythm of your breath kept time in a way that mimicked my lurking pulse. It was a painfully drawn-out experience. Right then, I was forging the memories that are now part of your myth, and in the middle of that night, as desolate as the city is desolate, a vast act of remembering set sail through my memory. The towers of that ceremony spread across the plain of my imagination and I saw how you opened yourself in flames, how you spun within the quartz of intelligence: a vortex of fire. If only that fiery birth could be contained, suspended. If only time in your dream could stop, could cup itself, like the convulsion of a moth caught in the warm hollow of a cursed fist, like the groove that the devil's gaze cuts into the blank page of reality. If only I could have had you like that, at the exact instant when the shadow disappeared from the face of the sundial, that midday in which your awakening marks the moment of ecstasy, and everything, except for your gaze, was like the essence of absolute silence, and that essence alone spoke those same luminous words as are spoken by the stars, the unequivocally distant stars, then I would have possessed the key to man's fate. A perfect light, perceptible only in the desire that suffused your body like the light of glowworms, nothing more, because by the murky light of the cosmos in the shadow of those ruins the body of your dream and the dream of your body revealed to me a secret that froze the blood in my veins. I moved closer to you. I observed you so closely that your breath fogged my reflection as in a mirror, and my consciousness became cloudy, like a landscape glimpsed through unpolished glass. Somebody should have written your name in that vapor. An unknown finger should have scrawled you there to commemorate the moment that that illumination struck me, by your side, and threw me into confusion, like a worm cut in sections, feeling the dust of the ruins coat my eyes. A paroxysm of horror, wisdom, and sinister desire seized me. The night in all its magnitude fell on my back like the shit or vomit of a crazed god. Worlds, galaxies broke over my head like a giant pisspot, and my teeth yearned to sink into something marble-hard and penetrate it as if it were rotten fruit. Without looking at you, blinded by a horror that denies everything but the feeling that the expanse of this world and the bottomless depths of death are entangled with one another, I slithered like a vicious snake, sniffing at the emanations of your abandoned body, and felt you sleeping as one feels the breath of the executioner's ax on the back of the neck, a pain like a dagger of light whittling at the eyes of the dead, the dead who lie sprawled with mouths gaping at the malignant splendor of the sun. When at last I laboriously sat up, so close to your body, I realized that my own convulsions had caused me to fall down. My death instinct made me reach my hand toward your body, but before touching your flesh, a voice, maybe my own, spoke these words aloud to me: 'The universe is a dream. She is the Fire Flower. Don't wake her.' A flutter of wings, like those of a nocturnal bird, echoed through the ruins. The footsteps of a ghost, perhaps, and I turned and fell on my face, by your side. The sad dawn rain revived my interminable wakefulness inside your dream, which, as I now understood, comprised our lives—but my eyes had lost sight of you. I looked around. Nothing. The desolation of the place suggested horrors even more tremendous, but also more rational, than the revelation I had suffered there in the middle of the night. As I shook off my sleepiness, I discovered X at my side. His silence was always significant, and likewise his words were incapable of making me forget my revelation. Dawn wore away as we trekked silently through the rain, arriving finally at a ruined portico where we took shelter. I'm not sure whether X witnessed my revelation, but now he casually shows me a piece of amber, in the center of which can be seen, with absolute clarity, a mayfly frozen in flight, which is to say, the suspension of an action begun fifty thousand years ago. Do you realize what this means? Is X aware of the significance of this information obtained after fifty millennia and reduced, at last, to a single, pathetic piece of matter? You are the mayfly: 'Break me; I am but a weak reed in your fist.' A gesture, a look, the convulsion that provokes a secret thought, a barely perceptible contraction of the ciliary muscles, rescued from one's mortal continuity by the enveloping pain of a gob of molten amber. 'Don't break me; contain me. Set me here that the world might have an eternity rather than a history. Tell me no stories—stories always have an ending with which the characters disintegrate, like bodies into carrion; don't turn me into a character in a novel, into the vehicle for an outcome that is necessarily banal because it is an outcome in which what once was simply ceases to be. Photograph me next to the portico. I want to stand as an immutable testimony, the harmonious memory of one moment coming face to face with another. That's it. Do I look okay here? Yes. The sun is at your back and, furthermore, this inscription is perfectly legible, isn't it? I don't look disheveled? It's important that you have incontrovertible evidence of that walk. It had been raining. The fields of hemp surrounding the cemetery were wet because it was raining at dawn, wasn't it? We'll make a copy for X. Is this where he showed you the piece of amber with the little fly? That was a special moment, a very special part of your life, don't you think? Of course, it isn't easy for the others to understand. An insect imprisoned in congealed amber? Bah! Who would believe such a thing? Yes, that's right, it's still flying.' But X had sensed the mystery; otherwise, he wouldn't be showing me the piece of amber. He showed it to me with the intention of starting a conversation about our conspiracy. He despised H, who was capable only of reading a purely intellectual meaning into the words that emerged from La Perra's dream. X sensed the essence of flight, the abysses through which her dream flowed, the gallop of a white horse on the plain, the secret relationship between her body and the exact location of the tabernacle wherein the identity of the Pantokrator will perhaps be revealed. 'You have traveled through a distant memory,' X told me. 'This desolation has made you forget the first stages of the discipline: the voyage, meeting with the brothers, the precise ends pursued by our academy, the disappearance of our leader, the enemies who lie in wait for us in the darkened alcoves of arcane libraries; but above all, you have forgotten our conspiracy. You ignored the intelligence we collected, and now you find yourself confronted with a prone body, with a dream that is dreaming us. Why didn't you come to the meeting we arranged at the foot of a statue, under the foliage of an enormous tree? What's this memory you're so determined to tell me about, the one you say you've forgotten? Maybe the key to all this dementia is there. Maybe that's the principle that governs the destroyed labyrinths at the outskirts of this abandoned city—and there's nothing left of it now but a trace.' I show him the photograph. In it you can see a woman standing next to the broken face of a sundial with some illegible graffiti inscribed on it. It has been said that the inscription was perfectly legible. That it is a sentence referring to the nature of time. X knows what it says, but he doesn't tell me.

'It's impossible to decode this inscription,' he claims, having had the photograph in front of his eyes without really seeing it. This is how I know that he knows what's etched there. 'We'll come back, you and I. We'll make a rubbing. Someday we'll know the exact meaning of these words.'

He leaves. I go back to sleep under the portico. In my dream I determinedly invoke the vision of La Perra. She doesn't come, but again I hear the words she would have said: 'Break me . . .' Why? Against a background of tedious violence I see the machinations of my brothers, all that hectic activity, which, in the bosom of Urkreis, never quite comes to fruition; all of them rushing around a figure that seems to rule with its gaze. He will be our leader. A man whose eyes we actually have yet to see. An absolutely spurious character in this book. The terror inscribed in my dream assaults me: 'If La Perra stirs from *her* dream, the world itself will dissolve in that awakening . . .' A strange paroxysm, inexplicable; it subverts the sequence of images, and I watch myself watching a sad spectacle that develops on the unstable stage in a tent full of acrobats and traveling magicians: 'And now the dance of the Fire Flower!' says the voice of a disturbing meneur. A ray of sunlight strikes my eyes, the first to break the veil of cloud moving away toward the mountains; the last image of this scene is an immensely bright light; I am awakened by the brilliance of this light defamiliarized by the terror of the dream, and by desire; a most sacred desire gnaws at me in the memory of that dream, burning my skin; more furious still than the pleasure that might be stirred by even the most infinitely aesthetic meeting of the flesh. 'Years later,' I tell myself, 'he who foretold the banal epic that still imprisons our exiled souls will return.'

But years earlier, in the protohistory of this myth, I was already aware of all the images that are now coming into focus like unreliable memories. After the rain, the morning coalesces and I roam among the ruins trying to reconstruct my hope. On the horizon, over the ocean, where clouds accumulate as if summoned by some remote and majestic design, I see the darkness of a distant night rising, streaked with the reverberations of feeble footlights and the presence of a tiny cathedral of memory. That was when I decided to search for the chasm that oozes certainties, certainties that later subside into the total fallacy of the world, causing life itself to become a chasm swarming with howling words. Then the memories called my name and the flimsy horror wielded by all secrets lost its hold on me. But in this book, that is an eternal present toward which all temporal perspectives flee, and these, of necessity, are more than three. The tortuous discovery of an infinite number of words, heard in the glow of those miserable footlights. The Know-it-all trained me only in the most rudimentary stages of the discipline of forgetting. I cried out to give myself entirely over to delirium; I invoked the worst kind of demon and I assumed, not unreasonably, that that conspiracy of incompetent acrobats and magicians was withholding the secret of the initiations which, in my memory, have already claimed the life to which they were destined. Because the dance of the Fire Flower revealed something more than gyrations, something more than the essence of a body that moves hypnotically through space; because it revealed the commotion of bloody sex, I sensed a ceremony. That's it. A ceremony. The ceremony of ice cracking under the rays of the burning sun on a savage coast. In the Know-it-all's words, little by little I discovered the connection whereby atavism rules certain fundamental aspects of our condition here. Throughout our pilgrimages to demented places, the Know-it-all had taught me this much: nothing. I even began to confuse La Perra's dance with the architectures dreamed by E, our dreamer of libraries, museums, operating rooms, and cathedrals. I knew then. He had invented an eternal and meaningless city. It was a city that could be read like a book. Now, in the desolation of his dream, the words of his tortuous descriptions resound like a tired echo. The only thing that mattered to our association was the anticipation of a ceremonial secret whose words were bewildered by formulas drawn from the least reliable ranks of knowledge. What I didn't know then was that perhaps I was E. Or else I would have been, had I been able to write that book; the precise account of facts contained in a notebook with a red leather cover, whose pages recorded a myth: the discipline of the Fire Flower, performed only in the last stronghold, a secret rift in the world which contains the world. Our first sign was an inscription, the one that appears in the photograph. X and I went to see pseudo-T, who was trying to decode the paleography. Perhaps La Perra had already spoken with him before we found him in the cemetery. He was lying on a tomb, inside a crypt, trying to decipher an inscription on the underside of an arch.

'I already know it,' he said, after we showed him the rubbing we'd made. He glanced at us indifferently, barely troubling to turn in our direction. 'I already know it,' he said. 'It's the inscription on the sundial.'

He spoke as if he himself were dead. As he spoke, he stared at the incomprehensible glyphs inscribed in the vault of one of those traditional Spanish monuments. Then he said:

'There isn't a single reference to any order that would make it possible to deduce the meaning of that graffiti.'

Pseudo-T didn't say anything else; but you knew that he knew the meaning of the inscription. No matter. You know very well that the opinions of pseudo-T no longer mean anything. It must be assumed, and always kept in mind, that his decoded interpretation would have been radically misguided.

E, on the other hand, was determined to bring his plan to fruition. The type of thing which, whatever the case, only happens to people with a strong propensity for fantasy in regard to long-term projects. He had glimpsed a city whose mental construction took up almost all of his energy. But you're lying to me, you say. You're lying to me all the time, with those myths of vestigial cities and whatnot. You don't care about me but you ardently want me to take part in this experience, in this discipline, in this madness. That's what you tell me. Don't forget that I've known you for a long time. Ever since you first passed yourself off as the Fire Flower in that little tent of traveling miracle-workers. Listen, Perra, I've known you for a long time, he says. La Perra has gone forward a few steps and he seems to be pursuing without ever being able to reach her. In fact, he pursues her like Achilles follows the tortoise. Isn't that so, Perra? That I'm going after you like Achilles pursues the tortoise? She stops and turns. Listen, he says, you know the Academy is being persecuted. If you don't give yourself over to us now, the project will fail. Until then he had followed her like a dog follows a bitch in heat. Also, he went on to say, you asked me to do it. La Perra had turned around to look at him, but he couldn't discern her features, since the sun was in his eyes and La Perra's silhouette rose in front of him, against the light, like a black sphinx. The words came from some indefinable part of her body.

'You have failed,' said La Perra. 'Things began to happen that hadn't been foreseen in the red notebook.'

'No, no,' he says. He blinked his eyes nervously, trying to find La Perra's gaze. 'Everything is foreseen; you'll see that things are going to happen just as we had anticipated them.'

'No,' said La Perra. 'It's later than you think.'

I advanced toward that radiant silhouette, which rose before me in such a way that I couldn't make out its features.

'We just need to decipher the inscription,' I told her.

Before I reached her, she exclaimed:

'Bah!' And then, like a plant, with perfectly surreal slowness, she turned toward the sun and kept walking.

I remained there, immobile, until she was out of sight. A shadow sun. That's how the twilight was; a dimension of perception by which that black, fusiform star descended to the end of that dusty road as she walked away. The sun, the other, temporal sun, clearly rose at the end of the road. Its elevation was corroborated by the noticeable decrease of the area in shadow, which, when they stopped to talk, had been much longer than when she moved out of sight. I then decided to go and speak with X, to explain La Perra's reluctance to submit herself to the experience that had been anticipated at the end of the text in the red notebook. I walked around the ruined buildings, recalling E's dream, an evidently unrealized dream. The old words echoed in his ears; the breeze wearing the fallen columns away: a grotesque, worm-eaten imitation of magnificence, which, in fact, consisted of the words used to express the dream and not the dream itself. The city had been conceived as the culmination of a supreme clarity. According to E, even the night would have been granted that blinding splendor of huge bonfires on the plain. Those had been his exact words . . . a blinding splendor. The morning was exceedingly bright, as if the rain had turned to light. Still, daybreak was devious there, next to that demolished wall where he had woken up. Dawn burst through slowly, as if it walked with the stealthy step of a killer. E had been able to describe the imaginary origins of the city with admirable precision. That was the ability he tacitly invoked so as to be accepted among us. It's obvious that absolutely everything was a lie. A lie concocted without the slightest skill in concocting lies. 'The city still lies awaiting its completion . . .' This phrase, although indicating excessive ambition, is likewise the product of an overwhelming fantasy. He also says: '. . . It's worth remembering the dream that erected the first structures, defying both the sea and the mountains that surround it as ideal borders around the plain upon which, like a dreamer made of marble, the city still lies awaiting its completion . . .' It's useless to emphasize the rhetorical character of this type of verbal construction. Seen from the sea, he once said, the enormous buildings that constitute the city, in their harmonious intertwining, resemble a net made of straight lines in which the weft is like the continuation of intermittent waves breaking against the cliffs in a howl of foam, and the slenderness of the warp fades and melts into the rising mountaintops behind it, guardians of its luminous solitude. Who could have designed this grand illusion of voluminous stone and seemingly endless space? What is the reason for the blinding light that encircles it like a magnificent halo? Who dared to limn the ethereal and unshakable prospects that devise and plot the city like a radiant and perfect crime, committed suddenly, in the form of an unexpected projection of towers, of rhythmic colonnades arranged in accordance with modules which simultaneously defy and gratify the possibilities of reason? Who could have dreamed—on a totally still night, beneath incredibly clear stars—the Firmament like a celestial orgasm, like the rush of all music toward the darkest depths of the sea? Whoever dreamed it has perhaps applied the hidden principles that govern the course of life—the essence of the laws that shape the universe—to the construction of this city with which the night commemorates the secret that is the life of men. And yet, farther toward the bottom or the very heart of the light that envelops it, the city stands like an enormous, winged declaration of darkness. In this silence—animated only by the throbbing of the remote sea, by the repetitions of that sound in the distance—the lurching, rhythmic pulse of time can be heard. In his dreams he watched the extension of that plain, which unfolds with the softness and languor of a woman's body, through the pine forests in the foothills of the mountains and the cliffs, against which the ocean persistently crashes. And he thinks that on such a night he must come up with a grandiose idea, and what besieges him that night with its somber, lunar clarity is the field in which the seed could thrive, as if it had accidentally fallen in a furrow; his mind, the main impulse for creation is in his mind. Thus did he contemplate the night and so many unthinkable geometries, like the breath of infinite connections that moves the stars, the stars that guard the significance of the task that has been imposed on them and which would have made up a cluster, a luminous organization of prisms in which everyone might watch the destiny of their tribe reflected— although in reality it would have been only the representation of a fictitious configuration of a supposed fact, kept inside a hidden cell where those who succeeded in entering would see a mirror reflecting not their face, but their fate.

The city would be the final destination of the world's every migration, a city planned since the origin of every nomadic people, its architecture would be like the reflection of thousand-year-old regressions, the crystallization of and end to every impetus to travel, the port of every ship and the end of every road. Thus does he dream it, and as he continues to dream, the city takes shape in his mind. The general order of his design gradually becomes a reality; the contorted inlets into the mountains, the vast bays appear before his eyes, but beyond his dream, hidden beyond the images from which this vision of the city consisted, there grew the idea that could have guided a project all of us would have undertaken at our own risk; this being, of course, a plan that could only ever have taken shape in the realm of ideas. He knew very well that the angle of incidence is always the same as the angle of reflection, and whoever might have contemplated the city from one of the two hills on either side of the bay would have understood that all the structures were an infinite series of reflections, and that the city itself was like the reflection of a reflective aspiration, which, by sheer violence, visibly spread and caught fire in order to be conceived as such, in the middle of the night, by a man who, perhaps, if it were not for the fact that the city itself was like a compendium of everyone in the world's desires, might never have dreamed it. But the city was also a reflection of his own passion, and, on the mysterious level of worldly things, his passion was foreseen by someone who, this very moment, also in the middle of the night, maybe on a rainy night in a landlocked city, conceives that other person who conceives of coastal cities: the secret architect who arranges the structure of the city with the same self-controlled ardor as a chess player who, over the course of the game, keeps changing the arrangement of his pieces on the board, until he makes the move that will grant him victory. And so, when he achieves checkmate, he dedicates each piece to the unseen gods that favored his victory. E had witnessed the birth and slow growth of the chasm in her eyes and he knew that that image contained the primary architecture. He thought that cities should grow at the same pace as mountains and that architecture is chaos reflected in a mirror that puts everything in order; that construction is ultimately just the emotional organization of matter. Which is why, when he first saw that vast plain surrounded by mountains and sea, that expanse of marble and basalt that entered the ocean with wedges made by gigantic cliffs that descended to rectilinear beaches at the ends of the bay, he could not help but throng it, in his imagination, with views, with towers and plazas. Why? Because he, who was also a nomad, had wearied of wandering and fervently wished to anchor his dream in that harbor bordered by the enormous breakwaters he had imagined: friezes in which the grandeur of his delirium was inscribed in the alphabet of a new writing; because if the city had to be on the margin of history, then it would contain all of history; it would be history. The architect's forethought would have taken this into account, and he would have given the city the feeling of an architectural museum in which, freed from death, forms of architecture from all eras would sprout up again, endowed with the life their inhabitants lent them.

This was the order of ideas about E's project that came

to mind while walking to the plaza, where I met X again. On seeing me, the first thing he did was show me a small piece of amber. I took it and looked at it closely. There was a little fly inside it, clearly visible.

'Fifty thousand years ago this mayfly was imprisoned in the amber,' he told me. 'What do you think about that, eh?'

I explained La Perra's attitude to him and returned the piece of fossilized resin.

'"It's later than you think,"' he repeated, as if to himself, as he stared at the amber he held in his fingers. 'It's your fault,' he said, turning toward me for an instant, 'but it doesn't matter; it's still possible to carry out the experiment.' He pointed to the piece of amber in his hand. 'If you say the words needed to melt the amber,' he continued, 'the mayfly will be released and it will fly again. The successful completion of an act begun fifty millennia ago: the act of fluttering about wildly for a few hours before dying.'

I didn't understand what X was trying to tell me by that parable.

'Come,' he said, motioning to a place situated nearby, 'let's walk over there . . .'

We went under the shade of an enormous tree. It was the only one around. We stopped beneath its leafy crown and from below the foliage, for a few seconds we listened and watched the panorama that encircled us. With one arm folded over his chest and the other extended at eye level, X made a circular gesture that alluded with perfect legibility to the landscape surrounding us, and said:

'We need to talk—' his expression, thitherto serious, became suggestive, ironical '—right?'

The question he uttered was the answer to a question
that always arose about the possibility of a metalinguistic
communication, which was like its own mirror image.

'Let's tell ourselves stories about things we've never done,'
he said. 'Imagine a beautiful verbal adventure, one that
has never happened, an impossible love, eh?' He laughed,
remembering some of his own experiences of that kind.
After a moment he nodded his head and, staring at the
ground, he said in a faint voice, 'Eh? Why not? Why not
an impossible love? We all have our defects, right?' He lifted
his head and smiled, exposing a row of uniform little white
teeth.

His smile had a disturbing peculiarity: it was a static
smile, a smile that never happened. 'Eh? And you? What
do you think about all this?'

Barely an instant of significant silence, then convulsive, somehow tragic, laughter descended between us like
the madness of communicating vessels. We were invoking
something with that grotesque laughter. I think it happened
because at that exact moment the landscape was like a text
already read with infinite pleasure. X knew how to avert
those belletristic moments. He became serious once more
and added indifferently, as if wishing to disguise his words
as a truth infinitely more important than what they actually
expressed:

'I often think that the world is an alchemical fact,' he
smiled. 'You too, right? A *fata facta*, of course, right? This
is how you have to understand the book.' He started making the circular gesture again, but faster than when he had
begun speaking about us as a literary image. '. . . I think that

character is a wizard,' he said then, referring to the author of the book in which we were supposedly characters.

This time he held the static smile for a long moment, and finally, suddenly, it exploded, it expanded, it broke up, turning into a painful guffaw, barely perceptible, almost banal. We were silent. It was a silence like a cistern being filled with unsuspected convictions. Unexpectedly, I experienced the sensation that a stone experiences on being carved by a sculptor. This, of course, is an approximate image, vulgar, too, but there's no other way of standing before a mirror, of being written. And maybe even X himself didn't know that.

'Eh!' he suddenly exclaimed. 'I don't know if what just happened to me happened to you, but it seems to me that the thing we just felt has perhaps already been written. After all, why shouldn't it have been? There are a lot of people who are capable of achieving such levels through writing; a previously read text . . .'

I was laughing at him in my mind. Silently cracking up. It was exactly the same kind of laughter that he had brilliantly organized just a few minutes before, while making a claim that would have been despicable from the start, but as we shall see, this is of particular importance—especially here.

'We might be like a novel,' he went on, 'a cheap and unimportant novel; one of those novels which, not without malice, you read in certain bourgeois houses whose inhabitants are not without atavistic refinement, those houses where it looks like dusk no matter what time it is and which have beautiful fruit bowls. You get what I'm saying, right?'

It seems as if I know his fantasies by heart. They're always centrifugal and expansive. La Perra has to appear now, I think to myself.

'. . . Rooms unambiguously inhabited by female forms . . .' continued X. Then he adopted an ironic, mocking tone, '. . . in spite of the Chardin! Of course! The Chardin that's hanging in the little room upstairs and which, on October thirteenth of every year, the day that's being written, is struck full on by a golden beam of light, a light which, at exactly six twenty-three in the evening, shines through the lucarne on the opposite wall. There's a woman in that little room. She has her back turned. She's sitting on some kind of couch. It's impossible for us to know who she is. The woman is reading a book. A book with a red leather cover. She doesn't pay much attention to the Chardin. That's fine. If she raised her eyes from her reading for just a second, we would vanish as if we were imaginary, we would recede into the air. The book that the woman is reading says that we are those two men, X and the other, who converse in the shade of an enormous tree. An aura surrounds the image of the reading woman, an aura alluding to a certain fact that makes her a part of this series of images that comprise the book in which we are being written: the fact that in this house thought forms part of the decoration, as if the support for that Venetian light were made of a highly rectilinear, Doric material. And amidst all of this there is only a vague piece of considerably absurd information.'

X stops. I know what he's going to say. Her hair. But no; he refers to a fact infinitely more important than her hair, unmentionable, even; the result of sharp observation and the application of a significant knowledge of biomechanics.

In the picture, the woman appears at the moment she begins to gesture. The tilt of her head in relation to the surface length of the pages, all of the supposedly possible natural axes according to the direction of her gaze, in accordance with the angle of the axes of her hip, of her spine, her cervical column, and the vertical posture of her skull in relation to the ideal vertical posture and the variable horizontal development of the parts of her body around those axes, suggest that the woman has come to the end of a page in her book. The impossibility of deducing the page the woman is reading by the position of her body, seen from behind in the semidarkness, puts us in an exceedingly sensitive situation. In fact, the entirety of our existence is implicated in the gesture that the woman has started to make and which almost no one imagines could be a gesture reflected in a mirror. You mustn't think about it, at least not for now.

X stopped again to catch his breath.

'The other possibility,' he continued, 'is that the book the woman is reading contains nothing but the description of the gesture she's now making, which happens in accordance with the description of the gesture happening in the text of the pages of the red leather book.'

He paused again and then continued speaking pensively.

'. . . Although it might also be assumed that one of us is writing the book,' he said, 'that one of the two of us has imagined all of it and has it stored in his memory, organizing it bit by bit before giving it a reality more suitable than that which writing can give it.'

He looked around. Without turning back to me, he then said:

'. . . I, too, have thought up a few novels. I've even drafted a few manuscripts. I have one which, like this one, is about two men chatting in the shade of a tree. They were two men who imagined themselves exiled from a perfect city and invented memories of places, of events, of women they had never met. They were in the habit of meeting there, under the huge tree, to rifle through their memories, as one might rifle through a bag, and make them ring out like falling coins.'

The images almost always show a *moderniste*, or at best Pre-Raphaelite, proclivity. I would have liked to speak with X about the ageless quality that certain sculptures have, seen on an imaginary trip to Florence, in the company of La Perra. This is the tone that turns us into fictional characters: the tone that sounds like everything is foreseen. Perhaps because everything transmissible is transmissible only due to its banality. We're interested in the other side of the coin. Which side? The other one. X and the Other . . . not the secondary figure that appears in the left of the photograph; not in whoever took the photograph either or in whoever imagined the scene of the two characters who have a conversation beneath the shade of an enormous tree; none of them, but only the Other, who remains silent, as X recounts the novelistic episodes he had once planned to write and which the other is perhaps carrying to completion. Right now. And this is what the parable of the insect trapped in amber means. We agree, X and I; the writer melts down the amber while imagining the flight of an insect that has been liberated and starts to move again after fifty millennia.

That gesture, barely hinted at. The strange tenacity of the

light, right then: October 13, 6:23 P.M., in a house in the
city of Polt. All these things without a doubt help to establish an atmosphere of total malice around what's happening
here. X says that he can almost hear the woman's voice when
he imagines her. He says that he can hear her muttering the
words that form the book she's reading: '. . . six . . . twenty
. . . three . . . pee . . . em . . .' X reminds me that we have a
meeting that evening. He silently walks a few steps away,
but suddenly stops and turns toward me, waving goodbye.
I watch him slowly disappear among the whitish ruins. I
remain beneath the huge dome of foliage, which rustles
softly in the wind. It's noon. Walking in the distance, X
casts no shadow in the dust. The Other remains immobile
in the shade of the tree. His presence next to that gigantic
trunk evokes distant dreams. He starts to walk around the
tree slowly. Pensive. Imagining sequels, brief, legible shocks
of life that formed the novel that friend had begun to relate
to him; the one about a woman who is reading a red book
in which we are contained as images. The total image, which
includes two men described in the moment they imagine a
woman reading a book in which we are the story, also forms
part of another book, but a book that is being written at this
exact moment. The reader of this book might ask: What is
that other book about? That book is about a lot of things;
but its essential nature is the description of internal subversion. The central character of the book is a writer who
believes in the possibility of achieving internal subversion.
He advocated the *ars combinatoria* as the only valid principle
of composition. Our author was familiar with literary styles.
That's why he even spoke of *moderniste*, Pre-Raphaelite

proclivities, etcetera. He is a character vaguely connected
with a photograph and with a story about conscious tele-
phones that autonomously call their customers. A gruesome
idea, if you will, but useful for containing the story within
an enigmatic limit. I remember, for example, the description of a piece of music heard over that telephone: '. . . in
the horns you hear the premonition of a heroic deed with
which you can't help but sympathize. . .' He ended by saying: '. . . an impassioned joy, irrational, but in some ways
geometrical, too . . . ,' after mentioning something along
the lines of a 'cataclysm of the senses . . . to which you aspire
. . .' The character hurls down the receiver and the connection is cut. There is a moment of revelation. The character
and a woman called La Perra had embarked on a joint experience of knowledge and feeling. On several occasions, the
author is left to assume that the character dutifully writes
down every detail of that experience in a notebook with a
red cover, although it's not entirely inconceivable that in
that notebook the character is writing an extremely banal
fictional chronicle about the tribulations of the members of
a society dedicated to philosophical studies upon discover-
ing the true nature of their activities; but who knows? It
describes the nature of the character's thoughts. The night
overflows with a dull imbalance, and there, in the book, life
takes the form that's been dreamed of. Does this mean, asks
the character, that I'm dreaming you? It's as if the world has
emptied out. Persistent breathing, with a rhythm and timbre reminiscent of the way sound emanates from a cello. A
contralto voice. Then he started writing in the red notebook: '. . . that it be called *The Secret Crypt*. Break me, said

La Perra; break me, I am but a weak reed in your fist . . .' A
gloomy search for solitude behind these words. He watched
her sleep. She seemed to be wide open toward that secret
underworld of life which, at the beginning of his book, the
author promised to describe to us, after presenting himself
as a character fundamentally at odds with the phenomenal
world. 'That antagonism,' he says, 'could not deprive me of
the spiritual commitment that I will have made to a few
ostensibly lost causes, but which are really just hidden until
someone, somehow, registers them in the chronology that
rules the mind.' Such, of course, was the character of the
events that took place and which resulted in our affiliation
with Urkreis. Our inventions have little impact on the
inception and development of our total desperation. I've
also dreamed in accordance with these rules. Situations that
seem to occur by chance, staring me in the face, just like
that. Expressions of reality revealing an unsuspected and
unsettling mystery—that was the prevailing desire.
Expressions that are almost always incomprehensible.
Grimaces in which the devil lurks, like lizards in a crevice.
We would all reject the conditions of such an agreement, if
we hadn't already inadvertently accepted them. You have to
take into account, however, the terrifying possibility that
we are being observed, that all of our secrets are known by
somebody; because every secret act reveals a death wish, and
reality's greatest gift is when it reveals to us the meaning of
a mystery. Tonight will be propitious, maybe. Our determi-
nation to capture meaning has led us to commit certain
crimes against wisdom. I look around. It seems like the
exact middle of the desert, and nothing—neither books,

nor flickering lights, nor the scars that writing carves into the whiteness of the paper—nothing has a tangible meaning that can be expressed in words. Old familiar objects, the familiar rhythm of breathing and the creaking of furniture, the settling of the Earth's crust, sighs that might have escaped from a dream, words that tell of ethereal pain. A still body near me, a familiar body. In the distance, perhaps ships. You are as if enveloped in a mist of tranquility, and your hair flutters about in the night, tossed by the breeze, which then disturbs the papers on the table. Notes regarding *The Secret Crypt* and the letter from X about the strange universe he has envisioned. By your side, on the windowsill, is the ancient instrument. A rocking of boats on the horizon. The cries of the jibs flitting about hunting phosphorescent fish. The impatient grunts of sleepy old sailors who await daybreak in their dreams. The infinite sadness of dawn at sea. As if the mist had frozen, as if the sun had never existed or was a hazy memory. We are made—such is clearly understood at night—to fill the void that the gradual death of things opens up in the mass of reality. Construction is the emotional organization of material, E would say. He wanted to be able to dream a city, as if by doing so he was building it. Like I build you in a dream, in that dream that X explains to the other in the shade of a giant tree. The Other. But who are you? You who dream about me? What do you dream? You dream as if on the edge of an abyss of total stillness. You're like the material that illuminates darkness itself before the sinister fluttering of that hair. A mysterious mutual understanding of space and time, as if the present becomes distant when I look at you. You have shed all of your gestures and now you're not capable of responding to any invocation. I call you in vain; I invoke you because I can't evoke you; I'm unable to retain the memory of all that you still are, there between the pages of the book that you were reading this afternoon, a book with a red leather cover that perhaps fell out of your hands, sliding off your lap when you fell asleep. The memory of everything that you will be later, a few pages further on. I turn and look around. The familiar facts of our common reality are in every corner of the house. They possess a sacred horror, like when something is about to be forgotten. Common objects, those little amber artifacts, the words that existed at the time, from that time when we were the sudden realization of an anxiously desired presence, a cessation of absence, a premonition which takes place abruptly, like X's laughter in the shade of the giant tree, which later another laugh, more inward than his, erases. There were moments back then when you would have wanted to be the mother of everything in the world, but the days, the corrosive process of the experience that we have embarked on, which maybe we have embarked on, have made our language incomprehensible. That's how you get to the point where it's necessary to think about death constantly. I watch you there, as you rest. The fatigue of all of these rituals has made you unreal. You seem as if you're empty, dead maybe. Above and beyond your presence, the first, faint reflections of a frozen dawn begin to glow. Because of the ambiguity of the light, it may seem that it's sunset. Perhaps you're dreaming that I'm writing you, that I'm recreating you through the words that my hand traces on the page. Maybe you're dreaming that you're one of the characters in *The Secret Crypt*, which, they say, is the story of a dream and of a character that dreams it. You're like a dream machine. I merely have to insert a coin into your wound to participate (via the lithoptikon, of course) in your mental pictures, in your dream which, if decoded, would reveal a secret about me that even I didn't know existed, unknown in your ultimate depths. That's how we would know the precise nature of those orgasms. It would be possible to schematize them arithmetically, and reproduce them experimentally, by means of stimuli from a different origin but with the same result. We would obtain total interpenetration of cause and effect, the line that divides before from after. An instant, no more; the memory of your look like a huge albatross settling on the buildings, as if on the sails of a ship, in the afternoon, when the light, after a loud and sudden rain, becomes gold over your body. That's how it went. Perhaps it was the same day they took the photographs. You could have spoken to me about confused zoos where the visitors are put inside iron cages to be admired by wild animals that prowl freely around the park. The essential difference lies in the tone of the gaze. The beast wants to discover us; we want to know the beast. Once the meaning of those igneous glances is revealed, the whole spectacle will seem banal to us, like the photograph in which you stand next to an incomprehensible paleography roughly engraved on an architectural fragment. Close to you, to your right, behind you, somebody's hazy silhouette can be seen. That's why I love to watch you when there is little possibility of actually meeting your eyes, such as when you sit next to the window and read or dream of new architectures. You

look like you're asleep or dead and after all, my vigil is made
of meaningless phrases; but there are times, at night, during
nights like tonight, when the words suddenly recover their
meaning, and so now the night becomes the ultimate night.
You are a shape, a form, nothing more, imagined from in
back of you, next to an oval window that sheds a beam of
light over a painting. I imagine you reading a book with a
red cover. You're like an illusion of words. The timbre of that
tenacious telephone takes you back toward the darkness of
your interminable dissolution. That incessant voice; the realization of a presence that rules our most secret acts: '. . .
have you heard that saying? Yeah, right? The night amplifies.
It seems to pulse with the rhythm of blood. Seventy beats
per minute. Impulses so violent that they gradually subside
into an unbroken pitch, a pizzicato, in the low ranges, con-
tinuously, as they say. You think you know these forms, but
you're radically mistaken. What you know about music
doesn't suggest, not even remotely or obscurely—you have
to consider that proximity and clarity are knowledge—what
music really is. It's a question of asymmetry . . .' And as you
read me in those pages, I write the book in which you also
are contained, reading me, and almost by accident, I fulfill
a vague project: the telling of stories. It satisfies me to think
that I'm still capable of maintaining the discipline imposed
upon me before the events that thwarted the aspirations of
our organization took place; that of completing the tasks
that this chronicle imposes on me, in their anticipated con-
clusion. I hope that the peripeteias of the plot that continue
to hatch as the book is written don't preclude the possibility
of finishing it. I reread E's description of the city. It's

deplorable. It has a stiffness that becomes wooden in its grandiloquence; but like a violent attack at the beginning of a symphony, it might work to establish the obvious stylistic differences of the arcs forming the development of this book of reminiscences, of dreams, of murmurs in particular. Sometimes I think that it's so hard for me to write it because I'm too preoccupied with trying to resolve certain conflicts that don't really transcend the limits of rhetoric; but it's good for the discourse that we know the exact form of our passions. That is, in a sense, what they call the act of creation, don't you think? It seems that the author would like to play with every possibility of the words. But yes, that desire corresponds to our urge to be distracted, by someone, something, in the most violent sense of the relationship that presupposes the worth of the active over the passive. It's necessary to live life, insofar as we're able to do so, in the same way as we write a novel. For example, right now I am writing a novel about which I know nothing. I only guess at the general outline of the plot. It's about a writer writing a book. However, what's important is what this book is about, the book the writer is writing there, near a woman reading a book with a red cover in which the writer is written in the act of writing this book. Of course, it shouldn't be difficult to guess. Were the writer writing a novel, it would be sufficient to know how old he was in order to know exactly what his novel was like. If it were a fantastic story such as the Chinese philosophers invented in order to illustrate their aporias and paradoxes, it might be said, for example, that the novel is about a writer who creates another writer, but one day realizes that he is the dream of his own character, who dreamed of creating him. I could only escape that dream by dreaming of myself, of me, Salvador Elizondo, whom I've invented as a character in an improbable book called *The Secret Crypt*, which, to put it rather more vaguely, is about a man and a city that have never existed. The man finds himself connected to a woman with whom he has an experience of a singular nature. The man tells the woman the story of a writer of fiction who has invented or might have invented or will invent both of them, the woman with the black hair and the other who watches her furtively from here as she reads that he watches her furtively while she reads and to whom he tells the story of a writer who writes a novel about a writer who writes a novel in which there is a woman who is reading a book in which he appears as a character who spies on a woman fitting the description of this scene, which appears in the book the woman is reading and which, there is sufficient reason to assume, is not necessarily this book, as some might assume, because ultimately that story, the one in this book, turns out to be a horror story, a story of sorrow and magic, if not even a story from one of those novels read in houses that smell like fruit, or not even that. Something like *The Begum's Fortune*, but in reverse. A sad story, but one which, in a sense, makes people laugh. This can be inferred from the event narrated in *The Secret Crypt*, where, on seeing her climb down a crumbling staircase, the character says: You climb down in the shadows, down the staircase, like the city descends from the foothills of the mountains toward the sea or like vultures swoop into vast ravines . . . And she replies:

'When you say that to me, I feel like I'm a character

that some obscure writer is inventing . . .' She hesitated a moment, as if she had forgotten the exact word that would accurately define the act that had given her a precarious existence within the pages of the book; the precarious, but unquestionable, existence of a fact made real by words. 'Yes,' she said, suddenly, '. . . a sad story to make someone laugh.'

"WRITING A BOOK IS, in a sense, rereading. The text builds itself out of its own repeated reading. A novel's true essence always arises from the writer declaring war on himself, on whatever he is creating. The composition is simply the misunderstanding of words and deeds, the misunderstanding of them in time and space, a misunderstanding that is its own identity. Perhaps I have described, throughout an imagined book, a woman reading this book. She's near a window. The only certainty is that her presence is real. It would be necessary, then, to know the identity of this misunderstanding that persists beyond the conviction that inspires it, and, also, to know the order in which each of us is consecutively registered and described by the other, in the other's dream— in the dream of the character that writes me writing about him in his book. If I suddenly had an abrupt revelation in which I recognized myself as the other's character, and I recognized that this other could be real, could be the true Salvador Elizondo—who is not I as I am but rather the pseudo-Salvador Elizondo—and as such, if I tried to write a book in which I might conceive of another, of the other who would be the character in the cosmic novel written by a god, I would be writing me to myself. But then, too, the window, the painting, the inanimate objects that occupy this space; the voices and the bodies of the voices and the voice of the other that speaks for the memory of others, the gaze and what it looks at, would all be the whim, the nonsense or necessity of a man condemned to write an infinite novel in which the characters are souls that remember; beings whose essence, ultimately, is words; the words that give a hierarchical structure—required by language—to feelings. But who has set themselves the task of giving us life? Who makes us their secret? A shameful secret revealed through the utterance of a word; a name spoken at the moment of death? They imagine that we imagine ourselves imagined. Now he imagines that I'm imagining you: it seems as if you're dreaming a dream about the substance that defines stillness. You dream your quiet life, sparingly—a life outside the spectacle. You travel through time with your memory. Do you remember the fluidity of that unexpected gallop, of that white horse on the seashore? A horse which, with its evanescent gallop, evokes smoldering fires. I urge you to conjure a memory and I would have told you: Remember the night when, for the first time, upon hearing that music, you experienced the disturbing revelation of our solipsistic condition. Perhaps someday we will have heard it? Only if we were the delirious text being written by a madman, by an individual with deranged mental faculties, as stated in document M-1273, and if that's what we were, what we are, then in the same way, that madman is writing about us, writing us, that woman they call Mía, a woman the author has invented, reads us, sitting on a couch, near a window. If we were those characters on whom the novelist mistakenly bestowed the memories of others—of the characters in another novel, maybe—and that were why we remembered that musical legato at the moment of revelation, if we were those characters, then the act of hearing that music would be a familiar and nevertheless alien experience. No, we are somehow more than someone else's dream. Or more than the dream that dreams our freedom, determined to fulfill itself in some way that transcends the narrow limits of a life in which love, the writing that we are, holds it prisoner. My hand is tracing these words that go on to build others, those of the dream; those words, in turn, are used to build me, as if I were the character in a confused, ambiguous novel. I want to stop. I decide to stop, to cast aside my pen and close this album that contains the chronicle of this experience, until another, more favorable time, when the words with which I write myself are less confused and ambiguous. And, still, there is something there; there is someone else who sees the written words first, who whispers in my ear: 'Keep writing; develop and distill the words until they become the hero of *The Secret Crypt . . .*' I open the notebook again and flip through the pages I've written so far, a small part of the story that makes up the plot of this book, and before my eyes I see something defined here as the word *window* and beyond *window* a purplish strip called *sky* and near *window*, I see *shadow*, perhaps *body*, over there, *painting*, and here, before my eyes: *album*, in whose pages I describe a man who describes and a man who is described and a described man who describes both and, as I write these words that describe a man writing himself, I think of the instant that the word was born and the instant just before its first utterance; that unique moment in the history of the spirit when the word was but the verbalization of the gesture, which is its origin, the fuzzy figuration of a universe of pure causality . . .

     'Did you say causality or casualty . . . ?'

"And that's how the image of the woman descending a staircase is built with words. Salvador Elizondo, or whatever the guy's name is, the one who came up with that image, compares her downward trajectory to the layout of an imaginary city that stretches from the foothills of a mountain range to the edge of a basalt cliff. It's an ephemeral image that gradually becomes clearer as the language develops and is distilled. That woman's identity will be made explicit. Her name itself has a hidden meaning which, as further words are added, will finally, at the very end of the book, be explained. Meanwhile, we know only that the woman is going to meet a man—her lover, perhaps—who has already described her with these words: '. . . like vultures swoop into vast ravines.' Or something like that. But who is watching them at the moment they meet? Could it be that perhaps an anonymous narrator, the secret and unknown author of *The Secret Crypt*, was hidden in the cracked structures that will make up the mysterious setting through which the plot of this novel wanders? Is he an unnamed character in the story, a name or an initial that the author has forgotten to record in these pages? Or a clever spy, a member of some antagonistic Brotherhood? Or a close friend of the Pantokrator, who has managed to arrive and who lies in wait, hidden behind a column, for the scene where she asks the man awaiting her at the foot of a staircase to tell her a sad story that will make her laugh? Or is he a killer waiting for the right moment to strike them down, both of them, in the middle of an embrace, and who later, on some desperate night, chronicles the details of his crime on a few wine-stained sheets of paper? Or is it X, on the lookout for an opportunity to seize some documents related to the lithoptikon? We shouldn't reject the hypothesis that the killer responds to the demands of a plan yet to be explained, or which Salvador Elizondo has vaguely invented so that, on the tragic night of his repentance, the confession of his crime becomes the only testimony to the meeting of the two lovers.

Another plausible conjecture: that those wine-stained sheets of paper have been casually ('Did you say "causally"?') found and then integrated into the corpus constituted by the codex called *The Secret Crypt*, which is contained in an album bound in red Moroccan leather and which collects fragments of a confused and ambiguous legend about a man who writes himself but doesn't manage to create a clear picture of himself.

'I can imagine a scene,' he says: 'A man writing a book. There's somebody near the window, opposite a painting. A telephone rings and from there, what? I know only that the man is writing a book called *The Secret Crypt*. It's a book in which paradox has a prominent position. But I, Salvador Elizondo, maybe I, too, am an apocryphal character created by the gods of literature. My character, that pseudo-Salvador Elizondo, who is simultaneously writing a novel and living his human life, imagines at one point that he is being written by me. But what proof of his existence does he have except the presence of that body, a body which must become tangible for whoever coexists with it in order for him to know that its existence is unquestionable? There's a part of the story where he, the character that is I, speaks of an album in which he is writing a series of words: *window, sea, painting, album*; he speaks of a character, a woman, who, maybe right now, has her back turned, near a window, and is talking about a musical composition called the Adagio. He's always just about to remember the essence of a memory; but the same as I, he doubts its authenticity as an individual existence exterior to the tale he tells. The writer who impersonates me in the pages of this book has something similar to what people call a Romantic temperament. A man who covertly invokes the testimony of a passion to provide proof of his existence. Perhaps that's why he, too, obliquely suggests the existence of a woman's body, imagined as seen from behind, near a window that is penetrated by a beam of light every October thirteenth at a certain time of day and which shines directly onto a painting that hangs on the opposite wall. The suggestion is so ambiguous that, really, it's impossible to know with absolute certainty if, in fact, that body is a woman's. It could also be the lifeless body of pseudo-T, lying on an ancient tomb that resembles one of those Spanish sepulchers with its reclining statues; or it could be the writer himself, having been killed by another character who hasn't yet made his appearance in the story contained within the pages of *The Secret Crypt*, or who has already appeared, maybe hidden behind a column, stalking the man and woman who meet at the foot of a staircase, but whose identity is still unknown. From a few elements, a story must be invented that, in the end, involves the totality

of the spirit. Maybe it would have been easier to write a
simple book, a book outside of pure literary creation; a
book that simply describes the life of men and women, like
all books throughout the centuries that have been written
without any intoxication or reverie, which is to say, whose
storylines are carefully registered within the limits of the
supreme fallacy that is reality. It would be a book like those
that are attributed to Salvador Elizondo, which never lack
an episode set on the seashore: the gallop of a white horse
on the beach, for example, or a dialogue that takes place
beneath an ancient portico, under the lintel of a mysterious
door. Important books require a liminal scope; a scope in
which the characters and objects are always, as in life, on
the verge of ceasing to be what they currently are, always
about to change names. The hero is named Ulysses, but the
moment he crosses the threshold of the beaches, he is named
Odysseus. He is another. Circe's lover is no longer the hus-
band of Penelope. He is marked by that spiritual tradition
of the journey in such a way that, even if Penelope doesn't
know it, the slayer of the Cyclops is other than the begetter
of Telemachus, which raises the possibility of formulating
an interesting conjecture: that Ulysses and Tiresias can only
be understood as if they were the same person and that
upon becoming characters in a story, all are essentially not
themselves, but otherselves. My character writes a story and
lives a life. He's at a point where reality, his reality and the
fantasy of reality I bestow on him, perhaps becomes confused. But literary critics reject—and they do so, of course,
for the sake of being beings whose purpose is essentially to
reject—the use that some writers make of words such as

maybe, perhaps, potentially, improbably; but the abolition of such terms would only correspond to the implementation of a univocality, of an absolute sense of words that would not only be the end and abolition of criticism's own reason to exist, but of literature's as well. All writing is the attempt to comprehend and convey a vision that is maybe or perhaps incomprehensible, maybe or perhaps incommunicable. That vision, which takes on the characteristics of hallucination in the minds of characters who narrate a story in the first person, that fantasy is, inadvertently, the awareness of a dream trapped in the shackles of wakefulness, which is to say, all writing is the realization of insomnia and literary creation an uncontrollable aspiration to dream. That's why, of all of the words that he writes—that I write, that the Other writes, the writer enclosed in the final cell, the isolation chamber, the imaginary writer writing me, the one that we imagine to be Salvador Elizondo, author of *The Secret Crypt* and author of this book—all we share is this album bound in red leather, this series of words arranged on paper in accordance with certain precepts that turn them into language and give them a deeper meaning and which are here being manipulated by someone who, in the end, is nothing but another of those words, a word which means nothing, a name which—although able to denote a specific person, accurately definable by an epitaph, as all names sooner or later are—is also someone, someone whose existence is doubtful, totally uncertain, and who would be indemonstrable but for a forgotten and remembered gesture, a gesture recorded in the form of words and which someone,

someone else situated beyond all hope of recognition and identity, has written here, on this page of *The Secret Crypt*.

"They call him the Imagined, and he is credited with founding the city. This conjecture is highly contaminated with improbability. It's one of those distortions that happen to the once-absolute nature of facts as the story progresses. The documents, of which he would have been the unquestionable author, would allow the formulation of laws that govern the structure and growth of ideal cities. As for the woman described here, it can only be said that her existence is vaguely recorded in a document possessed by the author. Aside from a few sheets of paper with handwritten autobiographical fragments, all I have of her is a curious pencil drawing whose casual style, along with a few words scrawled on the lower left-hand corner of the sheet, betrays signs of the physical distress of an insomniac coming to terms with her silent and exasperated vigil. When my mind is still, the Imagined tries—mostly in vain—to unravel the soul of the character who made those sketches, to decipher the hidden meaning of that naïve composition. I try to deduce or formulate a symbol for myself, a symbol that represents her with the feeling of those awkward sketches, of those representations that secretly aspire to be the revelation of a state of mind. I construct (why not?) a character destined to travel a tortuous path, tirelessly traveled over the course of a supposedly magical story, which I have fragmentarily glimpsed, as if in my indiscretion I had opened a door behind her as she sat near a window reading a book, and from this fleeting vision I could only deduce that the character is the embodiment of a myth whose origin lies in my own daily life. She is someone whose immediate presence dictates the acts of another being, one who carries out a fated mission within the language I record in *The Secret Crypt*; a being built in writing, whose appearance is simultaneously perfect and opaque, whose origin is uncertain, but whose fate, according to my will, has the blinding clarity of an obvious fact. In the novel, she will have to be that which is summoned by a visionary death: the secret thought of a demiurge.

X doesn't disagree with this. His novels have always been oriented toward the idea that it's only possible to verify the existence of the world if it consists of nothing but a series of words. When he presented me with a short novel he had finished writing, I couldn't help but think that it was actually a file taken from some confidential record, compiled at the highest levels of the Organization. It was entitled *The Uttered Man*. 'M-1273: Salvador Elizondo. Thirty-three years old. Writer. Fictional character in a book entitled *The Secret Crypt*. Our correspondent informs us that this person assigned ideas and programs to the Organization. On several occasions he has contacted by telephone a real person whose name he says is Salvador Elizondo, a writer who boasts of being the author of a tractate encoded in the language of metageometry, talking to him about the aims pursued by the Organization. It has been circulated secretly. This individual lives in the grip of a morbid fantasy that both he and the world in which he lives are narrated events.'

'This is a recording,' says a voice over the telephone, after a pause. 'It's highly likely that you were just listening to the Adagio. The calm cadences spiraling across the continuum, flowing back into themselves to disrupt and recreate themselves consecutively, within the continuum that draws in the slow introduction of the organ, right . . . ? Your current taste in music betrays a state of mind that's always approaching a violent break with reality—with the reality you had imposed as the principle that sustained a way of life in which fantasy would have been sacrilege. Now you insist on solving the enigma. You think that it's sufficient to write a series of words in this notebook to . . . But it's later than you think.'

"I guess that for a long time I've thought of men as if their essential individuality, what defines them, is nothing more than an agglomeration of words. I consider the universe a great, overwhelming dictionary; and the drama of everyday life, indifference, unpunctuality, the caresses, the feelings we feel that hurt or satisfy us, as if they were all—in the end— nothing more than the meaning that words are obliged to have. The universe, as we desire it, is a combination of nouns, of verbs, of adjectives; but this presence that seems to be here, near the window, how does it differ from the form it takes within the pages of an ordinary magazine? It's simply the photograph of a woman whom the camera converts into an inanimate object, via procedures that eternalize her, in a way: an interrupted gesture, a statue frozen in the act of uttering a word utterly devoid of importance. Where does the real person hide? Perhaps behind these words, like the fly peeking out of translucent amber.

"She leafs absently through a trendy magazine. Later, she leaves it on the windowsill, forgets it there. A breeze stirs the pages into a flutter of awkward convulsions. A face remains: it is the face of a female character: Mía, La Perra. She suggested that name to me and so I gave in to it; a figure of speech meant once and for all to deny me access to that other existence, the life that animates her. She walks away down the road, against the sun, without looking back at me, as the other continues to write these lines. Her hair billows in the keen wind, darting like a gust of daggers from among this ruined city's convulsive jumble of architecture. I watch her from here. I would have to close the album to halt her. She keeps walking and she recedes down the lonely path. That's what I write: she recedes down the lonely path. It's dawn, or maybe sundown. They're easy to confuse, particularly in those states of mind where it's difficult to distinguish the actual nature of time passing. I see or imagine her receding along a desert path. Maybe it has rained, or dawn's frost shines on the scattered ruins. Her shadow flits like a salamander across the dust, or like a drowned howl riding in on a whirlwind. I browse through this magazine whose contents occasionally excite her, and in which she foresaw an awkwardly etched inscription. In the back, to the left, the hazy silhouette of a man can be seen. He has spoken to me effusively of an evening gown—page 62 of a perfume whose aroma, fortuitously inhaled, always evokes a distant landscape of plains in the moonlight, plains which, almost imperceptibly, become dunes alongside an unexpected sea; of the notice from the telephone company—page 27 that warns customers against anonymous calls; of the photograph of a woman—page 103 the woman is standing next to a collapsed wall, among its remains one can discern an epigraph that has been worn away by the millennia. Her look reveals a perverse skepticism. The woman doesn't appear to believe that she is herself; she seems to be saying: I am someone's dream. Behind and to the right, the figure of a man can be glimpsed, but his features are murky.

That morning something occurred outside of the novel. X promptly appropriated it and used it in one of his little literary compositions. A novel that he called *The Anonymous Letter*. Under the enormous tree he read from it:

The Anonymous Letter

After reading it closely, Mía carefully refolded the anonymous letter and tucked it back in the envelope in which she had received it. She glanced at the postmark. It was too smudged . . .

"Diligently, I review the red album that contains the original manuscript of *The Secret Crypt*. Likewise, the notes on the book's plot, which are contained in so-called Notebook 9 and which will subsequently be called 'the notebook that went missing.' It's not difficult to notice the discrepancies, created by the novel's development, between the original plan, contained in pages 13–16 of the notebook, and what's actually contained in the album with the red leather cover. The synopsis, in its concision, summarizes a well-defined story in which the characters perform real acts. Almost all of them, including the city, already have a name which lends them substance in the order of writing: the city—that is, at least for the purpose of that initial sketch—is called Polt, and the female character is named Zoe. The book is devised on two levels; one is the life of the writer who writes the book, the other, the story he narrates. Through the incorporation of a myth, these two levels eventually become confused. The characters blend into each another so the myth can continue to build in accordance with a scheme concocted from fantasy, magic, and reality, like an exciting plot, at every moment guaranteed by dreams, madness, and solipsism that often betray markedly melodramatic and alarmist leanings. Some of the ideas outlined in the notebook actually persist in the album: the one about the telephone calls; the one about the photograph in a trendy magazine being tantamount to the origin of a millennially recurring myth; the one about the image of the man who is writing a secret chronicle in an improbable stronghold; the one where the universe is contained in an insignificant receptacle; the one where everyone is constantly and ubiquitously watched by an unthinkably vast police organization; the one where the bloody sacrifice of a woman is capable of redeeming them; the one where two friends talk under the canopy of an enormous tree . . . Each of them is an instance of the author's aspiration to render everything improbable, to make all identity ambiguous, including his own. There is no shortage of preposterous resources and demented formulas meant to create confusion among readers. The unknown voice on the telephone, for example, gradually becomes one of the characters in the book. In its obscurity and malignancy it is gaining a disturbing power and reality within my life. The mystery seems banal. Some idler playing an aesthetic game at my expense, and maybe at the expense of others, too. Indeed, the person who makes these calls has the ability to produce a painstaking a priori imitation of the most obvious figures of speech that the characters in this book would have used. Perhaps the inexplicability of that event, invariably recurring in conjunction with my favorite music whenever I listened to it, forms part of a plot that already exists and is already taking place, and maybe it is the realization of a plan that was hatched by another I, an ultimate Salvador Elizondo, that secret calligrapher who conceived of writing a mysterious chronicle, filling the blank pages of a red leather-bound album with our essential writing, hidden in the bottom of an inviolable crypt, and by whom I, a professional writer, a real, demonstrable man, am made maybe just an incidental word, insignificant, a hazy, gray figure like the one in the photograph, or like the voice on the telephone, nothing but an image, conceived by him as a literary game. Surely he, the he whom hitherto nobody has managed to give any name other than the Imagined, the he who is only an abstraction, smiled to himself when he created me to be conscious of that game he plays where he writes me into life. He would also smile to see me enamored of the ghost of La Perra, who is reading the book in which she is barely described, as if in partial darkness. Because everything in her betrays an unutterable aspiration toward the night. She is without origin and arises only in the words whereby she is written. A warm, soft terror emanates from her silent presence. She's like an image of Christ driven mad by its own beauty, an image that looks at itself in a mirror and suddenly understands that it is the fulfillment of a millennial prediction, the explanation of a mystery, the code whose utterance alters the only apparently unshakable arrangement of chance. Someone whose cause is writing and whose effect is reading. She rises like something that's being put into words and so exists; something described exhaustively, described until the words of which she's made wear out every possibility of every meaning and become an absolute meaning whose clarity is so intense that it redeems other ambiguities, and not just about her, but also the ambiguity of how nothing but a name was capable of opening those doors which, if they really existed and were not just the invention of a repeatedly incoherent and imaginative writer, would have imprisoned the enigma in which she, if she really existed and wasn't merely a character in a tortuous and necessarily confused novel, would have been explained as a form that is so unreal and so intense that here, in these lines, it becomes an irritatingly essential manifestation of reality. Something that is so unreal that it overwhelms the senses with its existence; a lie that is its own certainty. Mía is the demonstration of a statement that is or was herself, an idea that floods the night with weeping or laughter, and that sees everything with that vitriol-colored gaze. Nevertheless, there has to be someone destined for those crucifixions, that

testimony to a pain more real than even the discovery of
her body; more real than the certainty that the whole universe is eternal or instantaneously implicit in that flesh made
simultaneously to accommodate caresses and tortures, both
of which are like final statements about the significance of
all words. She is a word. Nothing more. A word that, if it
had been uttered lovingly, would have forever established a
night made of music and dreams; a word that will have to
stay forever fixed in silence; a word that descends a staircase
toward the heart of a dream where another, a stranger, will
have to utter it vapidly, like someone who responds to a
question which, in the end, is completely irrelevant.

"Of all the things he told her about the book, the only
thing that would have truly intrigued her is the part about
those two men speaking in the shade of a huge tree. The
two men who trade fictitious stories to kill time until their
persecutors, who must have noticed them, arrive. She has
to be able to visualize those scenes, those moments, in all
their detail, in order for them to reveal a well-assimilated
awareness of the essential concepts of descriptive archeology.
An idea distracts each of them simultaneously from their
conversation. It is a sudden doubt about their respective
identities. For both of them, it's essentially an ontological
paradox that can only be satisfactorily settled by returning
to the realm of sentient reality. I attempt the composition of
a fully realistic passage. Its language doesn't have a life of its
own, instead it's strictly subject to the conveying of an event:

the meeting between Mía and a character who could perhaps become important. The scene seems to be written in a linear manner, but, still, she emanates a feeling of strange anxiety. In the end I demolish her, and all I keep of her for this book are a few lines mentioning an anonymous letter, which X will convert into one of his novels: *The Anonymous Letter*. For the sake of the story, then, it must be accepted that she already knows what's contained in the letter. She is aware of a secret that only she and the sender know. Or also, maybe, the character from the deleted scene, whom Mía would have casually met one winter morning in a park—that is, if he isn't the sender. The contents of that letter are the beginnings of a conspiracy in which her subsequent fate is written: the possibility of becoming something like a symbol. The passions—that is to say, those circumstances of the human soul that subjugate the personality or body—always tend to turn those who experience them into archetypes or symbols. It's strange. That presence there in the semidarkness. That body that may soon gather itself up and go walking down the street, a fleeting vision in the early morning mist. That body is the first stage in an infinite process. A shadow that happens to allow the possibility of a caress or torture, and thus becomes word; from thence to possession, to total symbiosis, no more than a minute paroxysm passes, instantaneous, like a camera shutter, and the image stays fixed forever. Our aspirations immortalize an incidentally glimpsed gesture, a banal image, like that of the gold lighter belonging to the character described in the deleted scene. The possibility of total dissolution nevertheless looms over the immutability we believe our desire bestows upon life.

Death focuses our view of the world with painful clarity.

'God doesn't possess us,' he told me, 'otherwise, we would be immortal.'

What did he mean by that? Was it a way of accepting the rite? The gift of my death? We spoke of the hunt. Beneath fractured arches we chatted about the transcendent significance of weapons: Saint Julian's crossbow, Merovingian broadswords, and the mercies, the rites, the death ceremonies of fox hunts, the subtle manipulation of the foil against the most expansive of enthusiasms in a duel of swords. I remember the quiet, wooden atmosphere of those silent workshops where men toil to perfect death. The fire contained in the brilliance of glowing revolver parts that reflect light as if they were made of wine; that same fire frozen in the steel of those mechanisms whose clicks epitomize the perfection of metallic matter. We arrived at the idea that the animal state is purgatory. To grant death to an animal is to redeem a tormented soul. I want to be aware of her apparent and conscious calling for death. Like Christ. She says it to me in a language that transcends words. In her solitude she has begun to discover all these ignominious misunderstandings and now she has developed a passionate interest in *The Secret Crypt*. She believes, at times, that this is somehow a book that she is writing. She aspires to be an infinitely remote Christ subjected to an infinitely banal passion. She would have liked to see herself immolated in honor of a moderately wonderful ideal, cataclysmically futile, and I, on writing these lines that refer to *The Secret Crypt* as a literary work that is perhaps being written by someone else, ask myself to what extent it might be capable of satisfying her vanity: by killing her? By turning her into a character in this awkward story that doesn't really have any purpose outside of its pages, where, in the field that it describes and contains, we find ourselves, she and I, in the dark bottom of a stronghold where final ideas are settled and in which the universe lies abandoned like an insignificant toy in a cardboard box with rats prowling around it; or in an urban bar fifty thousand years ago, between two bitter cups? She and I are the only ones who speak of these things there, things that we, and only we, consider to be of significance. Ultimately, who knows if she is that woman who is completely indifferent to the end of the world. That's why she loves plays. She asked me to go to the theater and I told her that I didn't have time for things like that. I don't like to watch plays, I prefer to think that drama is a secret dimension of the universe; I told her that composing *The Secret Crypt* requires all my effort. Then she asked me to tell her about it. I told her the disturbing story of the two characters talking in the shade of a gigantic tree. Then she tells me about a play she once saw. On the stage, which portrays the foliage of a very large tree, two masked characters meet. They are identical. They discuss who is who. They fight over a single identity. Perhaps that of the Other, who never comes out on stage. She was undoubtedly referring to our own confused situation. Sometimes I think that she's the woman who was described, maybe dreamed, in the act of descending a ruined staircase; at other times, that she is the imagined, immobile presence, seated near the window, reclining on a couch. The character appears with her back turned. Like the rest of the characters, she is suddenly assailed by the ideas that I have placed in her.

In the middle of the night—insomnia. He labors to write those fragments that presuppose some totality situated beyond any possibility of realization. Just like he imagines her in his insomnia, she draws a picture, smokes disdainfully. Sometimes she turns her head and looks out the window. Outside, the night is a fundamental presence. As if everything that happens were founded in the surrounding darkness. Suddenly, it's incredibly clear, as if all of that blackness were the burning core of an immensely larger light that contained it. With that superior clarity in mind, Mía will have to consider a maddening possibility: that she is being watched from that other field where she, where her body, the form that she believed to be an unquestionable representation of reality, is not, in fact, anything more than the representation of an event that never fully occurs; merely a fringe premonition of her own present, a present that tends to go on forever in the pages of this book. This thought disturbs her because she has to believe that the anonymous letter she received—'You must show up . . . the interests of the Organization . . . a choice that certainly . . .'—confirms it. In the end she rejects the idea, but only because she thinks that she's starting to dream and she senses an interminable descent into the quiet and terrible world of a vision that will never leave her, in which her body will be like the symbol of a secret fact known only to me, her creator. Upon falling asleep she drops a sheet of paper on which she tried to resolve her finally vanquished insomnia. It is a naïve drawing, but one that astonishes because it emanates a huge burden of self-consciousness. All of the shapes and characters she depicts are a background upon which another reality is projected. Suddenly it would seem that there is a series of lewd figures as if fantasized by an adolescent, but it is an image ruled by a plan, by the laws of a rather abstruse system of symbols, because the drawing represents the reflection of an 'I' that looks at itself reflected in a mirror. A giant head dominates the composition, covering almost the entire surface of the paper—a sheet from a notebook—and above the head other figures stand out: naked bodies of women, a bust with enlarged breasts, a torso seen from behind, its right arm raised in an athletic pose. Stretching diagonally across the face is the figure of a naked woman reclining, with her head resting on her right arm, which is bent behind her neck, a leg is folded, and the work extends until it loses itself in its tapering length, off the edge of the sheet of paper. As if she were Atlas bearing the sphere of the world, another woman uses her arms to encircle the contour of the chin on the great face that dominates the composition; the ends of her arms blend into its flesh. The woman appears foreshortened, with her legs spread, the corners of her vagina are visible, and the face is given an intentional expression of pain or ecstasy. On one side of this woman, over the neck of the figure that serves as the background, there appears, executed in a less concise manner than the other figures, a classic representation of a human fetus seen from the front, with arms and legs crossed over its abdomen and its head folded over its chest in a vaguely self-absorbed pose. This motif would have led

me to believe that it was an indirect allusion to the lithoptikon even if its mechanism had not required the image
to be a cross section. There is a group of figures that form
a vaguely cathedral-like construction on the left side of the
paper. At the bottom, under the triangle formed by spread
legs, is the glans of a penis beside which flutters a butterfly.
A second image—which there was an attempt to obscure,
crossed out with nervous lines that were later smudged with
a fingertip—a virile shape pointing in the direction of the
vertex of the triangle formed by the spread legs. A vertical
shape, a sort of phallic structure is born out of this vertex
that becomes a cross. Each of its arms and the upper end
turn back into something reminiscent of the crossed-out
shape. The cross is a face and its arms give it the appearance
of a nun's headdress, and here, in this pained face, the representation of ecstasy is repeated   one of those saints who
give in to the contemplation of a disturbing vision. Over
the saint's chest Mía wrote, with a clumsy hand, in printed
letters: I CAN"T SLEEP. These words are underlined and
beneath the line is the date: October 13. The composition
continues toward the top in a circular tower shaded on the
right side to show off its volume. The tower is complete with
a conical roof behind which rises another, slenderer tower
that also has the exact shape of a phallus. Behind this tower
there is a naked woman, seated with her back turned and
shaded the opposite way, which is to say, as if the light were
coming from the right side. The figure seems to be con-
templating the view from the edge of the abyss beyond the
paper. An intensely sad, restless solitude encourages these
forms that allude to the desperation of a sensuality with

no outlet. At the top there are eyes watching everything, and in the middle, a body, like that woman reading a book near the window, who sometimes stretches in a voluptuous way. In this representation, there is flesh that cries out to be devastated. Flesh like a city awaiting the invasion of other flesh. A body that takes pleasure, like a city in the plain waiting for the rain to fertilize it. Her body is here, near the window. I move silently toward that presence, which, like the face in the drawing, presides over the ceremony of reconstructed experience. The pregnant, antique aroma of things that have been forgotten in the bottom of a poorly closed coffin—remains of a life long gone—the perfume whose aroma, fortuitously inhaled, always evokes a distant landscape of plains in the moonlight, plains which, almost imperceptibly, become dunes alongside an unexpected sea, letters never sent, the curls of her black hair, amber beads, an undated and unsigned letter between the pages of a red book. '. . . The Organization entrusted you with the clearest of all their images, but you couldn't tolerate a presence, a shadow. You would have wanted to welcome those images into your memory or your arms, the blinding testimonies of a desperate love. We watch you closely. We know everything about your life, Perra; your past is full of love and horror. We have a clearer memory of your life, infinitely clearer, than your own; we have learned to imagine you subjected to a tremendous caress. Everything leaves its mark on you. Your face is a sign and your flesh consists of a total anxiety over your fate. There isn't a corner of your body that we can't recite, as if your flesh were a story learned by heart. Nothing about you is alien to us. That's why you are the chosen one. You have to come . . .' She slowly wakes up, rises toward me. I close the coffin imperceptibly. She will ask me if I've been writing. She's keenly interested in how the composition of *The Secret Crypt* is coming along. She asks me anxiously about the final destination of the characters and especially about the fate of La Perra. Mía would like to participate in the writing of the book. She wants to be fully conscious of everything that happens in the plot, a plot whose dimensions multiply every night with the imperceptible speed of plants growing in starlight. She doesn't exactly realize who is writing the book. Maybe she is. I suggest this to her, indirectly. I show her a version I've made of an old sonnet about the strict relationship that exists between the author and his character. She suspects, not without some justification, that I was the sender of that anonymous letter. But she doesn't say so. I have pasted the drawing on page 41 of the red leather notebook. Now it forms part of this text in which our love takes the shape of secret writing.

"THE BOOK ARRIVES AT the dead end of a passage. The old ideas seem to have been abandoned. They move on, gaining new and notable characters, new developments in this plot that sometimes seems only to be developing for its own sake. The idea of the ideal city—a city designed exclusively to contain the development of *The Secret Crypt*'s central act—appears to have withdrawn into the misty depths, and it seems that anyone who gazed upon it lost all semblance of identity. Now the thread that guides everything to the final site must be recovered. We take up the original plan for *The Secret Crypt* once more. So it's an adventure novel, a metaphysical novel, scriptural, and in the same genre as *The Begum's Fortune*. Good versus evil; except good fights with the weapons of evil, and evil with the weapons of good, and in the end, I still don't know who would win, the adversaries being so infinitely matched. Perhaps rats would end up devouring the world. I remember the imaginary vision of the final scene in the novel that would have been; that perhaps somebody, in that world where only things that would have happened here happen, is writing, right now. An omnipotent police organization whose secret headquarters is situated in the city of Polt. Everything in that book had perfect intentions. The plot was concocted with the knowledge that religion was but a different type of mathematical equation. That plan required that at some point the reader think that *The Secret Crypt*—entitled *A Chronicle of Polt* at the time—was nothing more than an incoherent document, the product of a sick mind, the drunken dream of a tyrant. Some of the images would have evoked those blurred and sunless films about concentration camps. At other times, the age-old problem of the search would be addressed with the phrase *I am not responsible*, which always finds its way—by means of various clever documentation—onto the lips of tyrants, politicians, soldiers, police officers, kapos, gas chamber operators, those who incinerated the corpses. The book would have survived thanks to the application of a principle he had discovered but which he attributed to an ancient philosopher in the original plan. This principle proposes the abysmally intimate awareness of our victory over a world in which the opponent is but an illusion and where—in the end—everyone wins. The problem also arises in the rhetorical trick that now guides the primary course of action, narrated by one of the two friends who chat in the shade of a tree. Everything should have been as if touched by an extremely fervent sanctity. The characters were too inscrutable; so inscrutable that they were almost ignoble. They were police officers who meditated on the complex propositions of the *Principia Mathematica*, since it can be assumed that among the inhabitants of Polt there would certainly be men who possessed illegal and secret knowledge about the true nature of reality, and that these men would cautiously exercise their knowledge in an operation aimed at taking over the world through the methodical, systematic use of anonymous communication. That project corresponded, perhaps unconsciously, to the revitalization of a virtually forgotten dream, a dream that always revolved around the ominous personality of the Pantokrator, as this stranger, who we have all dreamed of being, is called: he who writes the anonymous letters and thus acquires, from the obscurity in which he feverishly labors, an absolute command over all men. It is true that, dispersed chaotically throughout the notebooks of Salvador Elizondo, innumerable observations, ideas, and possibilities relating to the composition of *The Secret Crypt* can be found. The original plan for the book has suffered some essential modifications since the day when Salvador Elizondo received the first anonymous telephone call, of which there exists a brief transcription in one of the notebooks, added after the original plan was prepared. The call refers to and approximately coincides with a few observations that were recorded on the same page as the ordeal of an explorer lost in the snows of the South Pole. The most significant idea here is to do with the tragic destiny of the explorer '. . . who accepts that his fate is to get lost.' Presumably, and despite the brief style of the transcription, the section was finished up to that point and the rest was reconstructed subsequently. '. . . *and Victory.* Perhaps believing that he had come close to something remotely alluding to an absolute experience. But this experience, in the second movement, might be solitude. Captain Scott, who experiments with the intensest of deaths. To die is simply to pass through the surface of a mirror which, in the [*illegible*] of the night, reflects nothing. Dying is just the farthest one can look into the mirror. Then the other begins. The god

[*illegible*] his reality [*illegible*] existence of men. It is what
he faces in the rear surface of the mirror when he looks at
it. We, on the other hand, are the manifestation of his need
to look at himself in the mirror. We are the props on that
gloomy stage that contains the terrifying gaze. In his case,
of course, it's a distorted mirror that reflects us, defectively.
Pain is the flaw that mars the reflection. You will say: Art?
Who does art reflect? And the art reflecting an artwork that
reflects itself endlessly? Think about it. We are nothing more
than pieces on the board of a game of *ludus latrunculo-*
rum; our future is the number of moves that we can make.
You have to burn that sight—which no one has seen—into
your memory, imagine it, persistently: Scott blundering
through a blizzard. You should take into account that in
those instants Scott can be seen or imagined only from
behind. He walks clumsily, blinded by the frost. Look, in
this twice-black night, for the glow of an azimuthal star that
is twice as remote in this double night. Eh? What do you
think? None of these things are totally uninteresting, right?
Surely the music will have made you think about it. You're
familiar—I'm sure—with the curious properties of certain
numerical progressions; like prime numbers, for example.
You remember, don't you? The interesting multiplications
and reductions that occur when you divide the continuous
surface of a Möbius strip lengthwise . . .'

"The organization summoned us. The time was auspicious
for a covert meeting. Covert because painfully obvious. How
can you explain a secret whose evidence is the most dazzling

tangible figure? Events were happening in accordance with a complicated logical scheme. Since it has been determined to be the fundamental purpose of Urkreis, the incredible structure of that manual—which at this point still consisted of the few traces gathered through the diligence of the brothers—will be rebuilt by our efforts. The great mathematical civilization of the species that preceded us in the history of the universe will be renewed by the application of those new alphabets, and the men who possess knowledge of those axioms will carry out phenomenal mental operations. They will make time stop, or they'll guide its course in whatever direction they want. But in the middle of those splendors of intelligence, the 'I' is revealed to be a desert island. Another project—perhaps connected with a fragment called 'Of the Secret Ceremonial,' which forms part of the calendric soffit studied by pseudo-T—attests to a special relationship that X and I have established, without really knowing it, inside of the wider relationships that constitute Urkreis. But just as X and I possess a mutual piece of information about the manual—a piece of information, incidentally, that the Zentrum doesn't know about—they, the rest of them, will be bound together in a similar community based on information that will secretly define other groups, which, in turn, may be embraced by the Zentrum. It's possible. And at the root of that project, as inside the innermost receptacle of a Chinese box, at the end of space, where the world of senses and notions ends, there lies a quiet hell, deaf to our symbiosis. The image of that ritual abandons itself to La Perra's gaze, as if it were her own echo; a murmur that precedes her, as in the experience referred to in Parry's canon. The fate that brings us, Urkreis, together around the same secret would suggest the invention of an imaginative writer, but we have to consider the possibilities of a certainty which, certainly, contains a curious conjecture: that the sender of the anonymous letter and the organizer of the telephone calls share a strange identity. Whereat the world's possibilities multiply, and this proximity to Mía is like the beginning of a journey with innumerable stopovers, toward a reality where this is but an arpeggio-like figure. What matters is the intimacy that she and I would have upon penetrating the successive layers of knowledge proposed to us.

She was already there when I arrived that day. The rest were there, too. They speak quietly amongst themselves. X says something in La Perra's ear and she turns to look at me. Her presence is suddenly solved, like an enigma. Everyone has discovered the cathedral of her eyes, something like the music of antique organs resounding in that bleak, frozen enclosure. The members of Urkreis, in muffled voices, suffocated, barely perceptible, subtly settle the final objectives of our organization. In confusing images, they explain the fundamental operations and, perhaps, unmentionable ends pursued by the cell. Those ascetic faces: I can only imagine them as a reflection in the depths of La Perra's pupils. Something like branches in her gaze, while someone, in the distance, describes Condillac's statue. There is someone who wants to summarize, for the person accompanying us today for the first time, the ends that Urkreis pursues. He speaks about the existence of a tangible factor in the attainment of those prospects, but he emphasizes the exhausting discipline that it requires. Someone else proposes that the

experience be carried out immediately. La Perra would have
been scared. She is scared the instant she sees herself enter
a subverted order of reality. Scared of being something like
her own kaleidoscopic image. We aspire to unknow the
world, says X. In short, we aspire to unknow the world.
That was what he said, and when he said it, it was as if an
ancient portico germinated on the featureless, pitiful walls.
X was sitting on the ground, leaning on a ledge, the way
the ancient philosophers used to sit in the Stoa or the peristyles of temples. They dreamed while leaning against the
columns. Another voice, resolutely imminent, will advocate
a method for making the substance of reality dematerialize.
A methodical oblivion. One of them addresses me:

'You aspire to wisdom,' he says. Then he points to Mía:
'She aspires to immortality.'

Yes. They postulate the possibility of police omniscience,
because all of their knowledge is inclined toward uncover-
ing the true identity of someone whose power has hitherto
lain in the unknown. He is that which is unknown. Terror.
They speak about it excitedly. Terror is a function of the
mind's helplessness, says one of them. Terror is only pro-
duced by the unknown, the unfamiliar. Someone else adds
that ignorance is an absolutely necessary method because
it frees us from guilt.

'In order to unknow the world, you must go on a pilgrimage to the source where that oblivion is born as if it
were the sudden idea of a god.'

Then someone else decides to analyze the problem of
ignorance.

'Which of the three executioners actually kills the

prisoner?' he says, concerning an old silent film. And then adds, 'It's impossible to formulate a question whose answer is inexpressible.'

Someone else says:

'We possess the answers to questions that the rest of humanity has yet to formulate . . . We're able to penetrate certain areas of knowledge that make it possible for us to make immaculate judgments. We can contemplate the universe from the other side of the screen and cross, if we wish, the threshold to other universes, to universes like the ones you describe,' he speaks to me, 'in the pages of your red notebook; those universes where only what would have happened in other universes happens; universes that are made of our retrospective suppositions; invented, yes . . . perhaps, but built out of a material made of loss, a universe whose very essence is the disappearance of everything that constitutes it. Home of beings and things that we will never again see; the irretrievable . . .'

Mía imagines that universe to be endowed with strictly funereal properties.

'They, the dead, are something we've lost,' she later says to me. Her voice ripples through our current world and her hierophantic life becomes evident. I look out the window at a fictional landscape—magnificent, enormous. A valley inhabited solely by light. The clouds play slow-motion morphological games in a seemingly infinite space. It's as if the whole landscape were a moment of total recovery, by looking, of what has been lost. From the back of the Academy, in a nook where the crepuscular light seems extra golden, a voice, just a voice, describes a technical procedure for

killing. The voice emanates from the very depths of a tragic
mask. A horrific fabrication echoing against the generous
landscape that I watch through the window. The voice and
gaze of Mía, lost upon my eyes, like an impassive wall, perhaps. I'm suddenly seized by the memory of that circus tent,
where the Fire Flower abruptly appeared on stage. Just to see
it. Everyone looked away, terrified by those eyes whose most
concrete expression was a form of dance. I think about the
discipline that will inflict on us the sought-after experience;
the discipline of La Perra's gaze in the night's severest horror,
always before the dawn's first light. The gaze is hidden in the
bottom of a well, below the deepest water; a complex tunnel
of communication with our apophatic and identical anti-
pode, invented by some evil or phenomenal geometrician.
Life is understood as a process of recovery then, recovery
through ignorance, of everything, of something that we lost
fifty thousand years ago. The rumor of death spreads like
music, and the man who voices it, recumbent on a step—
the image is fixed by Raphael in the frescos of the Rooms:
the thinker who can see himself sitting in the foreground,
on the steps, in front of the Athens Academy—says that
this is an argument he has meditated on for many years. He
alludes vaguely to a conversation that took place beneath
the foliage of a huge tree. A forever motionless tree. He
finishes by saying that it is necessary to mark an unstable
boundary between the "I" and the Other. And then the
discourse on those gardens beyond the window, the luxuri-
ous terraces of vegetation that puts nature to shame. She's
at my side. The realization of an undoubtedly instrumental
figure. Her mind will be as if filled with mirrors. She'll try to

distract herself, or to pretend she is distracted, by humming an amorphous tune until the Urkreis brethren mock her. I suppose she's exasperated by how slowly that speech about the source of the mask comes up, but she may also imagine that she's in possession of a little secret and smile to herself. She smiles at the thought of getting involved in such a crazy idea. She never manages to imagine that she is actually an invention, simply a word repeated innumerable times in the pages of a book called *The Secret Crypt*, whose author is a certain Salvador Elizondo, a narrator of precarious imagination. She likes to live with her horror focused entirely on those processes of reality that keep her body from exceeding its own limits. She shares her hatred, but she's surprised by her participation in the discipline. 'Maybe we're about to penetrate new levels of knowledge.' She smiled, as if the idea were wholly unimportant. Nevertheless, there was a passionate conviction apparent in those words, and her gestures suggested familiarity with ways of thinking that exclude the dialectical condition of the world.

'. . . . a purely discursive universe, where the dialectics of the world don't work . . . ,' said someone.

'Yes,' said someone else, 'I think of that universe as if it were wholly obvious that we are simply the prefix or suffix determining the condition in time of an absolute word.'

'Yes,' said someone else, 'all of the self-imposed discipline we've undergone will, with ideas aroused by the simple fact of the experience, perhaps help us understand the most profound nature of what is called "the real" . . .'

'A nature,' said the first speaker, 'that is sequentially evident, like writing.'

Then he made a somnambulistic gesture, which was remotely, but unquestionably, reminiscent of the act of writing, and finished by pointing at himself, index finger extended. This gesture contains an ulterior meaning. Everyone seems to know that meaning. They know, without a doubt, that it alludes to the possible condition of their being written by someone else, by a stranger, or by that other character in *The Secret Crypt* who is sometimes called the Imagined.

'Who is the Imagined?' Mía asked with her eyes.

That question, along with the enigma that it evidently encompasses, contains, to a degree that fluctuates only in the vividness of our memory, the same emotional intonation as certain nighttime landscapes. No one ever ceases to ask such questions in the moonlight. They look at themselves, sometimes, silently. He would like to take her hand. but he's checked by the image of a tiger, glimpsed briefly in the twilight. Its brilliant eyes shining in the architectural bays. Maybe they're undergoing a very subtle metamorphosis without realizing it, a mysterious transformation into another order of reality. He thinks that this order, the existing reality, includes an already-seen image: the photograph of a woman; and that reality, like himself, dissolves before the awareness that they, too, he and she, are murky characters in a novel written with a certain literary aim, but which is really in the same genre as *The Begum's Fortune*. The atmosphere of the enclosure admits a faint brightness, and the shadows bestow an unsuspected quality upon things as night falls. Language becomes malleable and now communicates only that which is clearly part of itself. They remain silent about anything that cannot be clearly expressed.

'But the material world disappears here,' someone says. 'It is as if we were facing the evidence of an absolute fact, but a fact that's also, somehow, ambiguous.'

It is as if they were occupied with the realization of a strictly linguistic dream. It is as if they had given up their fury and the whole night were now a silent festival. But X doesn't hesitate. His voice, always distant, says the words he knows La Perra wants to hear.

'Perhaps all of this is part of the love that we profess for the extinct, the unrealized,' he says, and then he adds that the story they are inside requires him finally to explain the nature of that coexistence: '. . . the methodical study of the origins and foundations of geometry.' Then he says that the implications of that search are extremely important in order to modify the constitution of the mind and allow it to penetrate the upper levels of knowledge.

'Why?' asks La Perra.

'To formulate certain ideas, which, although impossible to summarize in common language,' replies X, 'are realized the instant they're uttered and which, or at least the corpse they leave behind, are subsequently destined for tangible purposes, such as writing novels or stalking people . . .'

X stops. He looks at Mía for a moment. The meaning of his look expresses a strict relationship that once unfolded in some remote part of his memory.

'. . . You ask yourself,' he continued, 'what other reason there would be to devour the putrid and futile carrion of those thoughts that we can often only understand as the delicate existence of a barely enunciated beginning, grasped like a mother recognizing the first noticeable movements of an embryo in her uterus . . .'

He's not looking at La Perra any more. He continues to speak in an indifferent tone, the tone used to give technical explanations.

'. . . The ulterior motives behind those thoughts are detailed in a book whose existence we've already proven without ever having been able to see its contents.'

'But how do we know the book exists? It's possible that the book has never been written . . .'

Upon hearing these words, X smiles.

'There's no doubt that the book exists. Would we be here now? would we be who we are if the book didn't exist or had never been written?'

'But then why isn't it capable of telling us what we're doing, what the goals of this organization are?'

'Maybe because the author of the book, this book in which we are the characters, has yet to write the goals, or maybe the reader who is reading us has yet to arrive at the line containing the idea of what we really are. Or perhaps also the reader has already read it unawares, on an earlier page that has now been forgotten. On the other hand,' continues X, 'the aims of this organization are contained very clearly in our assignments to study geometry. Schematically, of course. Perhaps it's interesting that we should try to guess, through the hypotheses we keep on formulating, what the true nature of all this is . . .'

'But what about me . . .' says La Perra, '. . . what am I

doing here? I don't understand what you're talking about. If that's the goal that you're pursuing . . .'

'Try to understand as clearly as you can,' X tells her, 'the exact nature of the secret relationships that entangle everything in the world. The mission we've set ourselves, ultimately, is to gather all these codes. We'll transform ourselves with them. Our organization is extremely perceptive. Perhaps the author of *The Secret Crypt* is, in the order of our small universe, the mind that invents the characters—that invents us—in the book, and perhaps he has penetrated more of those levels that we've been talking about. He can see every aspect of us, just as most people believe a god sees us; with the words he's writing right now, at this exact moment, it is he who rules the course of our lives . . .'

'Bah!' exclaims pseudo-T, who has been drinking and hitherto hasn't said a single word. 'That's what you guys believe!' Then, facing up to X, he adds, in a contemptuous tone, 'Do you know what we are? We're clumsy actors playing out a boring drama on the decrepit stage of an abandoned theater.'

Pseudo-T thinks that by making this type of scandalous assertion, his presence here, in these pages, will be more significant. Sometimes he believes, when he imagines he's one of the characters in *The Secret Crypt*, that ultimately, we're something like a tale told by an idiot, an idiot incapable of even vaguely comprehending what we, his invention (the invention of an idiot), call sanity.

'Our author,' he says, 'doesn't understand us. We are the absurd creation of a god who doesn't understand anything about us; who only understands madness because it's his own nature, the same as we know our nature is polar and comprised of both madness and sanity. What's happening is that we're speaking through the masks that he wants us to wear.'

'You're wrong,' says X. 'He, that idiot, the author of our universe, he who babbles to us between convulsions and phlegmy discharges while watching the clouds pass by, that idiot in whose mind we are nothing more than the grinding of teeth; that idiot lives in a universe higher than ours; he lives in a synthetic and perhaps false universe, where the idea of opposition forms a part—as with the infinite correlative centers of a god who creates both himself and us—of something like a world composed of metaphysical curiosities, paradoxes and aporias, fleeting thoughts, rumors, banal advice, idle gossip like that which proliferates before and after huge catastrophes, in prisons and in churches converted into latrines, in the little vestigial centers that endure or will endure beyond the holocausts. The importance of that character who is supposedly writing us lies in the fact that he knows the language of the survivors and he knows that this book is written in code.'

"It is an apparition that occurs only at the very end of a desperate solitude. The figure is eternalized in a sort of defiant pose. A painter. We demand a less ambiguous description. Someone who is infinitely secret, but also infinitely precise. Someone who is formless yet tangible. We demand to know what she's like. We'll have to send for the Master. We want a conventional portrait. We want to know what La Perra was like. What was she like, then? What was La Perra like, X? Ambiguous in her unquestionable precision. So tangible as to be formless; I already told you that. We demand an explanation regarding La Perra. We have to send for the Master. We want a conventional portrait. Sometimes I amuse myself by thinking that she, too, in her insomniac nights, like October thirteenth, imagines the possibility that I'm a secret agent, even though I'm just a painter.'

'Excuse me. It's late. Yes, we know. It's late . . . This recording was prepared fifty thousand years ago in order to be transmitted right now. Please . . . Don't hang up . . .'

She interrogates me with her eyes. 'Who is this?' Fields of grass fill her eyes. 'Who is this?' She asks me through half-open lips. There is a definite quiver in that half-uttered question.

'Only the devil knows . . .'

'Ah!' she exclaimed. 'Now I remember. A few months ago, when you started to write *The Secret Crypt*, you wanted me to read a book because you had imagined our mirror image. The image of our love, which you wanted to coincide completely with images from a book where our love was described in terms of bloody surgery . . .'

The only evidence that the book exists is in her knowledge of the city of Polt's topography. But she's here, sitting by my side. Her eyes, the absolute swell of her forehead, indicate ignorance, indifference, or total disappointment regarding the nature of the mystery that has by now manifested itself to us.

'You'll be subjected to an exhaustive interrogation about every aspect of your persona that remains unclear. You mustn't attempt any of those arguments that criminals employ to make excuses for certain events, such as that you suffer from partial amnesia, invariably spanning periods of your life when it would be logical to assume that you were subjected to certain disciplines that would have been able to provide access to . . . No, you were wearing white and walking the hedge-lined path, wandering randomly, completely unaware that you were going into the last stronghold at the absolute center of a huge labyrinth, that center from which you always return with a dizzy knowledge—as complex as the labyrinth that contains it—of the construction and growth of ideal cities. Or do you deny having known, at some point in your life, the author of those confusing ideas concerning the structure that made it possible to deduce the module governing the growth of the secret, hidden cities contained within ideal cities? Did you hold him in your arms? If so, by seducing him during a night inhabited by geometric gardens, the tension of your climax would have revealed—that is, if you had woken up as he watched you sleep at the base of a wall after retracing an infinite number of meandering steps—some evidence of the Organization's plans. I would have told him, for example, that the essence of the entire labyrinth is the infinite number of labyrinths contained inside of whichever labyrinth. A maddening image if we consider that it perhaps sheds light on a mystery that has always perturbed the author of that book in which we are still just the unformed outlines of characters who—bit by bit, as he uses up the pages on which he deposits the pen-strokes of our life, like a mysterious universe contained inside one of his own insignificant reports—are slowly taking shape. Say it now; confess that you're aware of the prodigious revelation that has been given to us in the form of an enigma: the existence of a complete city from which it is possible to communicate directly with every telephone in the world. Ah! Do you see? What we've arrived at! A simple matter of communication. A matter that we've come to understand thus far as a concentration of vestigial cultures, where we assume lies, somehow at our disposal, the secret that the Organization has striven to hide. You mustn't dismiss the idea that all of this is but a phantasm, the transmutation of a type of philosophical dialogue into political conspiracy by reckless or irresponsible people who are trying to recruit us, you and me. I blame you for that loving communion, which now turns us, in the eyes of Urkreis, into a united pair, into a conventional portrait. The loving unity that exists in every novel. You know it. That's what you would have wanted to be. The main character of *The Secret Crypt*. That's what you are in the chaotic confusion where I reconstruct you. I've undermined your origins. I've written and rewritten this banal story. The story of a man and a woman who meet at the heart of a mysterious organization. But why were you there, Perra? Now we can speak comfortably. We can be certain that no one will hear us here.'

'What happened to the city foreseen in the first few pages of the book?'

It has drowned in the surging tides like a city built of sand on the beach. We live in the ruins of a dream. As for the city, E would have ended up admitting defeat. Murmurs. That's what we're made of. That's what this novel is made of. Don't be afraid to correct what I say. Right? That you and I had the same secret thought? A secret thought about the Pantokrator. Everyone had well-founded suspicions about this character's identity; suspicions that we intended to clarify. But we've forgotten the origins of our connection; our anteriority's command of over the events that would have narrated the novel had the novel been a work of pure and immediate narration; but the fact is that we still have to deal with the entire issue of those strange operations that were set awkwardly in motion by what happened in the tent, beginning with the final phase, when they had only two little facts that were, ultimately, for no real reason, totally unimportant. The game became dangerous when somebody, the person who writes us, certainly, realized that it was necessary to consider what those two men who meet under the crown of a huge tree are saying about us. X knows. That's why he's shared his little literary ego trip with me and shows me, every afternoon, when we meet up to chat under the giant tree, the ersatz novels that he furtively writes in his solitude.

'This little novel,' he tells me (it's barely two or three lines), 'is the description of a magical night when two lovers prepare to play a game, the game of love. They play and they fall in love. At the moment of orgasm, the world's ludic nature becomes clear in their minds, but to avoid facing a possibility that would put their true emotional condition in doubt, they assume an air of indifference and cynicism, and then they begin to play the game of death. All of this happens in a single night . . . Of course, you'll tell me, they're nothing more than literary images. Images, just like that day when we spoke in the shade of the tree about our literary projects and you were worried about the possibility of being one image among many. In which case our nature was totally meaningless if it lacked a plan. Instead, it is important to know the nature of the plan, to expose an act's skeletal foundations.'

Then he gave me a few yellowish sheets of paper, obviously torn out of a large format notebook or album—that's what the torn remnants of the seams showed, the classic seams of a notebook made not with hemp thread, but with silk thread passed through Campeche wax—a few yellow sheets folded in four, which had long slept with the dream of oblivion among the folds of his old tunic.

The Fire Flower, it says, in block letters, at the top of the document. Then the supple writing forms this pattern: *All of these things take place over the course of a single night . . .*

'It's about a game,' X tells me. 'A complicated game.

Everything. Us. A game that consists of deciphering the rules of a game that we've already been playing. A game that hasn't been invented yet, although there are those who have already lost.'

'Who?'

'The people from the circus tent. They wanted to play the game and so they invented the myth of the lithoptikon. An immense fantasy . . .'

X doesn't believe in the lithoptikon—an instrument capable of producing uncanny revelations.

'. . . Tonight,' he continued, 'we'll have the evidence we need in order to deal with the situation we find ourselves in due to the lack of interest among our members.'

That's what X said to me when we met again that morning.

'We know very little about the people from the tent. It's possible that the Know-it-all possesses information that we are perhaps yet to access, but this is part of the game we're playing.'

Who's playing against who? The Imagined against La Perra. They're playing a game called *The Secret Crypt*. It's a game in which the pieces are the possibilities of possible novels. The black and white pieces are moved around a black and white checkerboard, which the opponents try to dominate by various methods. The number of squares is always a multiple of three, which expresses, through its exact position on a Cartesian graph, the inner mood of whichever character is represented by the chips. The game is the only informative activity that consciously comes from us. La Perra already knew all of this. She entered the game knowing full well that the gambits were subtly prefigured by the Pantokrator, who perhaps already knew about the apparently aborted conspiracy that brought us out to these ruins so far from everything. The game was invented as an attempt to gain access to knowledge that will perhaps help accelerate the fall. But the fall of whom? The game will, naturally, have to result in an explanation of the significance of the last chip that remains on the board: the Commander's chip. But then let us assume that the Commander is someone who—being aware of the informative nature of the game we think we're playing with La Perra tonight—is prepared to prevent us from recognizing his identity; he knows, that is *if* he knows, that tonight we'll play the game that will reveal us. But H, the geometrician, had already told us; he told us that Urkreis was simply a society that lets its members practice playing games. Yes, simply mind games, which are of strictly academic interest. Of course, as his failure to finish his ideal city shows, E, the architect was, like H, a poorly trained dreamer, who left us nothing but these ruins, the remains of reports that other millenary migrations handed down to us, here, in some desolate spot near the sea. We're here, inhabiting a crevice, because, out of his entire dream, he salvaged only this indecipherable mark where we thrive in the dark, hidden, behind a sign that was created by some unknown person, almost always silent, like ants without a purpose.

"I was walking toward the circus tent, which had been erected on a grass field bordering the cemetery. X already knew what was going to happen. He had even written a little novel about it: '. . . not far from the cemetery, the lovers met, as lovers, for the last time.' That's what X's novel said. Their meeting under the crypt is disturbed by the arrival of an old man who tells them their own story, the story of two lovers who commit a crime in order to take possession of a mysterious instrument. Or the story of a ubiquitous character who, using the love of a couple of misguided lovers, carries out a sacrificial experiment called the rite of Herminester the Exhumed.

'Come . . . ,' I say to La Perra. 'Follow me; I need to speak with you.'

She walks a few steps behind me. Her flesh flits around me like an infernal bird. She walks a few steps behind him. He doesn't want to see me because he feels that my presence bewilders him like the fluttering of birds.

'It depends on you . . . ,' I say.

'Why?' she replies.

A conversation doomed to silence. He thinks. He remembers, step by step, the staggered progress of this plot—a plot apparently ruled by a pre-established program. But no. Everything is filled with a new excitement. I draw and erase you with each step we take along this dirt path. But no, it's not about all of that. Such things distract us. They distract us from the rite. From this.

'Look,' I say, turning toward her, the crown of an enormous tree in the distance, in the direction of the ruined city, reminds me of a conversation begun fifty thousand years ago. 'X,' I say, 'showed me a piece of amber with a flying insect trapped within it, frozen in the mass of coagulated resin.'

Unawares, we arrive at the cemetery. She makes no

response. Whenever we meet she is overcome by a feeling of distrust. She is confused. Maybe she's an agent sent from Polt, like so many others, to sow division in the structural system of secret cells, of brotherhoods that hide the identity of the Pantokrator. A conspiracy, perhaps. Based on a terrible mistake. Schemes that are carried out at the most abstruse levels of this solipsism. Better that we agree on one thing—she as much as I, we are both characters in a book, *The Secret Crypt*. She thinks that I am the author of this book and therefore know the identity of the Pantokrator, but she doesn't realize that *The Secret Crypt* is the representation of an absolutely gerundial universe, a never-ending plot that's being initiated every minute, without ending . . . yet. The author and his book are also being written, and although there is practically no doubt that Salvador Elizondo is our author, his authority is in fact questionable.

'It's strange,' I say, 'that one would work so hard to be something like a god, no matter how distant. That's why we have to live in a universe that is contained between the covers of a red notebook in which the entire world inscribes a little bit of itself . . .'

But she doesn't listen to me. She's lost in her own thoughts about the city that E once dreamed. The ruins in the distance, like the remains of a dream, still foreshadow its possible fulfillment.

'Look,' she says peering around, 'look at that city which was designed to be roamed by wild gods and our beloved dead. It's almost sepulchral, isn't it? That prodigious *ofrenda*, the ocean, for those who remain intact in their stillness, but who are fundamentally silent.'

The ruins looked as if they had emerged from some solar cataclysm. It was hot. We sat on the edge of a ruined mausoleum. In those words of hers, I can pick up the everlasting nostalgia of her body and see her disheveled hair. I'd like to cut a lock of it to preserve between the pages of this notebook. I'd like to take her in my arms and, as a means of terrorizing her, say that whenever she slept, she might never wake up again, if I so desired. I could kill her with impunity, disguising myself as someone else, as H, or X, or the Pantokrator, or the Know-it-all, or Herminester ille Exhumatus, who is an ambiguous character connected with the shady ceremonies carried out in the circus tent. Desire shows up like a pack of hyenas drawn to a pile of carrion. The afternoon sun falls upon her forehead. A narrow tomb of gold crowned by the dark brilliance of that hair. She doesn't listen if I talk about who might be listening to me in the order of these dreams, as they say. I caress her body. She doesn't listen. He begs, he implores, the beatitude of those words that are invariably an injunction to madness. There's something about all of this that seems reminiscent of those conversations that you have only in the visiting rooms of holy insane asylums. One day, she told me, 'You've written: "... *the continuity of everything within an order.*" But has it ever occurred to you that the order, and the god who establishes it, might just be something inside of a broader order, and that this broader order is your own absence? That this subsequent universe is entirely hazardous? Don't you understand that perhaps whoever possesses the key to that essential order of the world possesses, so to speak, the code that could deduce the governing law?' Right then, there was a veiled exaltation in her voice, as if someone else were speaking through her mouth. Did she perhaps evade the true goals of Urkreis? Is it really a vulgar conspiracy? I don't know. From that day forward we've always felt that we're being watched. To this, she added something else that one of the Organization's members casually asked: 'Have you ever considered, in the most impassioned paroxysms of your imagination, the possibility of seeing, without being seen, what the others do when they're alone?'

Ah! But I've inflicted a muffled violence on your body. It's a surgical violence in which the dialogue seeks to provoke a greater surrender than what you've already so generously given me. In those quivering moments your existence as a woman yearns to transform itself into the rigor of a militant discipline made of infamous commands, and just as you're obsessed with mirrors, so too you believe that *The Secret Crypt* is a mirror that reflects words and you assume that those words are slowly outlining not your figure but your meaning; the most secret meaning of your mindset when you open yourself infinitely to me. You open yourself like a bay dreamed by our architect, E, you open toward the magnitude of that vessel that is more persistent than any other vessel: the sea, which erodes and undermines you. That sea and that love which foreshadow the dissolution of all infrastructure, of all those precarious foundations, of the strength of every plaza and cornerstone. You shatter with love in my arms, like the most perfect scaffolding collapses to fragments under the abuse of the sun that erodes and demolishes it, always at the brightest noon. You would have been like those cataclysms, too; there is something

blizzard- and tsunami-like in you, in your voice, in the most fleeting palpitations of that voice which says, as you lie next to me between corroded fragments of buildings: I am La Perra. Why? Whose eyes are those? Whose eyes are those when you shelter me in your breast; when you say to me, 'See how I open myself to you'? And in the end, you're like that door, every part of you is like the door to an abandoned mansion. You like to talk about the anatomical configuration of a bitch in heat, and how you suspend your judgment about it. Your experiences can't be turned into ideas. They're senseless experiences and all you want is for me to take you as my own and you feel a slow cavalry, a fluid galloping across the plains of your flesh, right? You scream. You scream like barbarian horsemen scream and you spur on the words that you beg me to say, as if they were old horses, unable to overcome the rectilinear expanse of your interior steppes; that epic gallop of our universally intimate story; hordes that penetrate you and break open the borders between everything that you are and the adjacent possibility of everything that you could have been; the meaning of everything which—someday, once we have executed the secret plans that gave you life, plans that we now possess— you will be, as vivid as the sun, fixed in my gaze over the abyss, as immobile as I am in the convulsions of this embrace; an embrace that leads to a dream . . . .
. . . .
. . . .
hidden in the darkness, the Know-it-all had been lying in wait . . . .
. . . .

. . . . and now I think
of *The Secret Crypt* as if it were the narrative contained in a
banal story. The tedious story of suffering; each incident
contained in the album with the red cover as the final
moments of the author's life that he sees passing through
his mind just before death, obviously except those that refer
specifically to the final days of the Organization. The two
men who would have spoken of this under the tree have
refrained from commenting until now, perhaps because of
the natural impossibility of doing so if they themselves were
members of that secret brotherhood, the one whose members ensconced themselves among the ruins of a failed city.
Because of all this, it's reasonable to think that our author
wouldn't be wrong in making the character descriptions
conform to the rules of the old precepts, since the fact
remains that he has never been able to give an explanation
of what she, La Perra, really was. This is why, now that she
alludes to a secret that might include information about her
trip up to this point, she has to be repeatedly invented and
reinvented. The Imagined will try to describe Mia enveloped
in subtle circumstances that would cover the most profound
depths, of not only her own passion, but also the passion
she aroused in the minds of the persecuted who took refuge
in the ruins. the Know-it-all was certainly a witness-bearing
presence. Ask him what they did there. Ask the Know-it-all
if you want to know who they are, the final followers of
Urkreis. If you want to save her from that heap and redeem
her forever, if you want to fix her here, make her forever
motionless in the pages of your red notebook. Ask the
Know-it-all. He knows the whole story from the beginning,

from the time those rites were invented. Ask him if you have
a burning thirst for a more substantial picture of La Perra,
for a picture more substantial than identity itself. Or perhaps it's a trivial picture that doesn't deserve to be recorded
in these pages: the tone of her voice, the color of her hair,
the reflection in her eyes. The metallicity of her voice, for
example, denotes an unremitting tenacity for wearing out
every possibility of an idea which, nonetheless, hasn't been
able to define any other ideas that might serve to fill the
lacunae remaining in the manuscript contained in the
red-covered album. Is she the Fire Flower? You'll have to ask
the Know-it-all. Is this about the characters of a book yet
to be written, a book which, once it has been written, will
be called *The Secret Crypt*? Is it possible to ask the Know-it-
all about this? Do you see where we've ended up in our
desire to define, albeit with only a temporary clarity, the
limits of a novel in which the author talks more about himself than about the characters required by the conventions
of drama? What's it about, then? 'We need to outwit the
plans of that mysterious being whose memories we now are,
whose ideas we were,' La Perra once told me. 'We need to
get a life of our own. There are those who have already got-
ten one, in their own way. The people of Polt. The entrance
fee to that order is a life in exile from an entirely novelistic
fate . . .' Why novelistic? Because one day X had written
another of his little novels which he gave me in the shade
of the tree. This story was about a few characters, or maybe
just one character, a character who tries to escape the plan
X himself had devised. How does he escape? By penetrating
the silent spaces E had imagined as a world that comes into

architectural existence through use of the writer's failed material. That silence was the key to redemption for this character, who went on to live in the murkiest hovels of some imaginary, but definitely living, edifice. 'For him, I imagine,' X told me, 'a totally silent world, devoid of words and yet infinitely mobile in its apparent stillness. An entomological world of insignificant facts. In that universe the flight of certain birds is kept aloft by the symbolic manifestation of an infinitesimal calculation. Suddenly, however, there occur inexplicable moments of absolute stillness. In those moments the character imagines us: you, me; he envisions us speaking about him; you and I speaking about him in the shade of an enormous tree such as this; a tree that stands on the outskirts of a vestigial city, nothing more than ruins in the middle of a plain. In his mind, the image of a precarious species takes shape; clans who inhabit great plains studded with bonfires around which the exiles invoke and remember the apparitions of Herminester the Exhumed, clans whose lives rest on simply the same spiritual stillness and the millennial observation of the slight effects that sunlight has on the structure of the chalky buildings that rise almost imperceptibly and in whose crevices thrive solar salamanders, chameleons, and serpents. The language they speak is just the appearance of a language, which, I imagine, probably exists on another level of reality. The mere awareness of this fact, the awareness of the possibility of this encoded language, is what feeds those pariahs. At times, amongst themselves, some of them speak of us, of two characters who, in another novel, in an enigmatic, confused book called *The Secret Crypt*, talk about them in the shade of an enormous tree, such as here . . .' So much he told me. We'll have to admit the possibility of being characters in a story devised by a couple of tramps around a bonfire! And La Perra? Is she too the invention of some mad storyteller?

'Certainly,' he answered. 'So far, we know very little about her: that she descended a staircase, that she reclined on a couch near a window to read a book with a red cover, across from a painting, that she walked through the ruins of a subverted city; we assume that she possesses a secret extremely important to the future of our organization; we also suspect an infuriating relationship between her and the unknown commander. We have fostered, as they say, secret thoughts about La Perra, don't you think?'

I didn't say anything. I wouldn't have known how to respond, because, in some way, the idea that I had always had about La Perra, she and us, everyone, was that we had thitherto been merely someone's secret thought. But whose?

Probably the author of the anonymous letter that Mía received: '. . . her participation in the events that culminated in the dissolution of Urkreis, after which those documents would not be recovered . . . you must bear in mind that these drafts have been entrusted to you . . . Take the necessary measures to place these documents in the safekeeping of whomever is able to extract therefrom the most information for the use of those who cannot see them without using them improperly . . . you must go . . . without revealing to anybody the reason why . . . nor the fact that . . . the time has come to carry out the experiment . . . with the goal of investigating the final possibilities to which they refer . . .

would otherwise run the risk of being severely compromised
. . .' The foregoing, more or less, typewritten on ordinary
white paper. The postmark on the envelope is illegible. 'Bah!
It's totally incomprehensible,' she thought, hastily folding
the sheet of paper, replacing it in the envelope, and stowing
it in her handbag, which she had left near the bed. Nobody
is exempt from receiving this kind of letter. Speculation
about the origin of such communications is what impedes
our progress. For a brief moment, she'll suspect that I've
tried to figure out the contents of the letter she always has in
her handbag. One might imagine—readers should do this
on their own—the possibility that Mía is a woman placed
in a predicament due to her inclination—characteristic of
certain beings who are tangibly involved in situations which,
in reality, arise from unrealistic circumstances—casually to
settle questions which, while extremely important in the
realm of spirits, are not, however, accessible to the experience
of the senses. But no matter. Her presence, the final and liv-
able reality of that captivating appearance, would be capable
of retracing the steps of time contained, in the form of language, on pages 76 and 77 of an album with a red leather
cover. The instant her suspicion is aroused, she will formulate
a full acceptance of that reality which makes her own wholly
unlikely: the reality of that act which consists of describing
her eternally, but of describing her within an order in which
she is, in addition to the word that expresses her, a feeling
that aspires to the tremulous dissolutions of her dream's
silent paroxysms. Thus, she will perhaps suddenly scream
before getting past page 83 of that book she's reading. She'll
let loose a cry, which, like the mayfly contained in X's chunk

of amber, will be suddenly liberated; liberated and, nonetheless, contained here, on this page, on this line, in the
following words: Herminester the Exhumed is watching
us. All of a sudden, she'll say it, stifling a shriek. Perhaps
the red book falls from her hands and remains open at her
feet, open to other pages, fifty thousand pages further than
where she was reading or fifty thousand pages before where
her reading was interrupted in the instant when an indelible
memory, not a fleeting image, crystallized in her mind; the
form of a cry that couldn't cross the warm and secret perim-
eter of her throat, the ill-defined threshold of her tense lips.
That cry was an insubstantial foreshadowing of death; the
violent agitation of a final breath, beyond which neither the
body, nor the image or memory, nor the recollection can be
uttered or be part of a dialogue made of words alone. There
were the seeds of a dance in that convulsion, the gyration
of something that seemed to flutter slowly, imperceptibly,
around a brilliant, holy event where a will to ignorance was
realized, a failed attempt to forget. She then turns and looks
out the window. Turn back, slowly . . . imbibe the intoxicating pale light seeping through the windowpanes . . . Now
forget . . . Forget everything . . . Twist around yourself like
a reptile . . . Don't say anything . . . Maybe you don't even
exist . . . You're just a word spoken in the shade of a tree, a
hazy character in a story that methodically records the premonition or forgetting of things that are happening. Is that
right? You're capable of imagining her, of actually seeing her,
or am I wrong? She's still sitting there. The book has fallen
to her feet; it's open to another page; to a page in which
you and I are written as vague scribbles, voices under a leafy

tree in the middle of a plain. The final ones. Yes. Voices that
no one hears; words that delight in constructing the previ-
ous image of La Perra, when she remembers herself like a
somnambular fact; the realization of a dream that contains
both of us; words, too; that's what we are. Her black hair
is like the foliage of this giant tree in whose shade we are
the words that don't cross the threshold of her voice, the
lintel of her lips. The wind rustles the branches and hair, in
a slow gyration, it plots a curve, made completely of shadows, around the blind face of the dream; it's like a black
light that brilliantly illuminates the center, where beneath
the fractured vaults of mortuary crypts, the shining afternoon air brings out the skin subsiding after the ripple. The
Know-it-all would have wanted to put a crown of thorns on
that black fire so that her forehead would flow with other,
more accurate writings; bloody typographies that fall off the
cliff of her temples like small streams to satisfy his thirst.
Then, from the secret hiding spot whence he watches us,
he came up with the circumstances conducive to the ritual.
I tell her that.

'Perra, they want to crucify you.'

And confronted with that image, recorded in some part
of the manuscript that M-1273 is currently writing at this
exact moment, she wasn't worried; she told me that she
trusts in the mercy of the author writing us. X says that
it's about a game in which the players don't exist. X says
we're not the players, but the plays they make. Nevertheless,
under that light that turns brown in the cracks, her voice
is truer.

'Who am I?' she asks me. 'Who am I in this story?' she

asks me, as she opens her dazzled eyes after a light sleep interrupted by her consciousness of my body next to hers. I barely manage to sneak the anonymous letter back in her handbag without her noticing.

You're the story of my passion, I think. You're something that someone is narrating; yes, in the shade of an enormous tree; an imagined figure in whose characteristics, in whose gestures, in the absence of gestures and words, in the immobility and silence that emanate from a dream, I try to discern some indication of the metamorphosis which, the same as whoever imagines it, should be implied in her very existence; but I can't find that reality in her, the reality required in order to realize solitude, instead there is a fullness that exceeds the insignificant power of words. Sometimes, not in her eyes, which merely read, but in the worldly things that encompass her eyes in the writings of the Imagined, I look for the furtive relationship she has with the inner space established by this novel; I search her body to see whether they leave any trace or perceive the senses that perceive her and love her—and I don't succeed. Her existence will suggest only events that occur in the maddening realm of the imagination. That's where her story happens; that's where she resolves her unknown passion, the passion whereby she will have claimed a more inward and complete life in a mind that has been inventing me for the last fifty thousand years. It's a lonely stage of that reconstruction, of that redemption whereby the mayfly restarts its flight, of the possibility of experiences that will have taken me to the limits of death where the contents of life momentarily assume a luminous organization, maddeningly clear, perfect, before forever disappearing from the world of things perceivable by the senses and transmuting themselves into myth. Therefore, it will be about a disappearance to a level of reality that is less obvious, but infinitely truer. This transformation happens before the character disappears forever, like a body that has fallen into the hell of oblivion, cast there by the author in the middle of the book. That, of course, is a form of death—when the Imagined forgets us. So I'm reclaiming myself from death, like the sea claims from the cliffs a greater area for itself, eroding the rock foundation with its tenacity until a cataclysm occurs and the collapse restores a more essential kind of pleasure. He'll take her in his arms, and it will be like the moaning representation of a dream that will be dreamed with the same three-dimensionality as the white horse galloping on the seashore. The part of life perceived by the senses is like an angry mob; a mob that advances to the edge of the abyss that is us, overcomes it, and then tumbles over to vanish like an exorcised demon. It remains only in writing, in memory: the beating of hooves, an echo over the plain of the body, do you understand? Now you pass out. Absent from yourself. Now you're here with me, in me. Between you and me, Perra, there's a harmonious relationship whose violence kills. A star. You see it there, through the crack. Let's go; it's starting to get cold. It will rain before nightfall, I'm sure of it. Come, come here, next to me. Don't walk away. May the night fall on our embrace. You understand what I mean by this, don't you? The sorrow that appears on your face framed by the ruins is a false feeling. These are the moments that precede a deaf, silent communication. Yes, the pain, at such moments, becomes

so sharp that it penetrates everything violently, crossing the
limits of every abomination we imagine to be inscribed in
the most obvious regions of pleasure.

"'He'll take her in his arms," you say; but if so, when will
we have this ceremony that we've planned?'

'After that embrace,' replies X. 'After that pain. You still
don't get it? The ceremony can only take place in the stronghold. La Perra must be dominated beforehand; she has to
reveal the true nature of her relationship with the nucleus
of the Organization before we can know whether her revelations actually give us access to the experiment we intend
to perform. Then we'll discover her like a sacred continent,
an Atlantis conquered in a dream late at night . . .'

X's words seem to have a will of their own, and as such
they foreshadow the moment when the floodgates of the
night, of fate, will open for us, when the blackness and
horror will become luminous.

(I scream. I moan in the paroxysm of climaxing pain,
as if I felt the hand of Herminester poke at my eyes with
a burning-hot ember. I want to fall to my knees and revile
the gods. I want to pray a litany of blasphemies that would
drive him beyond his infinitely still words to bear witness to
this crime; I want to wallow in the slop of his threatening
gaze like a reptile in the bottom of a sewer.)

X erects a monument to the night according to that will.
I look around. The obelisk and the cloud are in the exact
center of a plain scattered with extinguished bonfires, erratic
colonnades of smoke. A wasteland that harbors the millennial germination of grasses, that shelters E's failed constructions, struggling pathetically to rise toward a sun that

will never shine on them, and always beneath the trembling foliage of this enormous tree, there is the incessant clamor of a criminal deity. The hierophantic nature of Mía's life suddenly shows itself; in the memory of her gaze I discover the persistency of consecrated stares. La Perra moans amongst the tombs, covering her face with her hands because she knows that he craves a greater terror. She has an insatiable thirst for darkness, and in that darkness her erratic eyes sense the corners of an obscure horror. Just as we remain ourselves, just as we take hold of the night with this love that we imagine stubbornly while fulfilling a bloody possession, our bodies, at the back of the tomb, sketch bitter emblems, tegumentary calligraphies which, as if it were what they are, contain only the signs that guide our steps along a painful path. At this moment we are the celebrants of a devious sacrifice. The Imagined summons us to a terminal rite as I go over it the same way one goes over a road on a map: with the point of a pencil that bleeds script. Now, on the levels of a strictly mental pain, we confront the exact nature of the experience we've been proposing for fifty thousand years. We have just started, she and I, to cross the threshold of a desperation that covers us as lichen covers the body dissolving in ancient pain. The primeval indication of this decline is already manifest in life. Barely perceptible. 'A discipline of forgetting,' she says. It is necessary, in order for her to forget, to keep in mind that the dream revolves around a possibility. The obliteration of memory. Remember and forget three times in a row the words contained in this book. Because, ultimately, this is about forgetting and remembering at the same time: remember a dream that only contains images that will be forgotten; or images of events that haven't yet happened and will only be contained in this book as a result of forgetting. The goal of the experience is to annihilate any possibility of actualization. When we've got that, you'll have discovered the secret depth of the enigma of *The Secret Crypt*.

To what extent had La Perra accepted the requirements of that discipline? It must be known with absolute certainty, using every bit of evidence they have demanded. When we reach the final depth, it will have cost us all a certain degree of death; our dissolution toward other, more essential, perspectives, because the fact that her existence inhabits the terrible whiteness of these pages doesn't alter the essential course of her story: her story is an interior story; already contained on other pages; the pages of a memory that's fixed through writing; an interior story that is playing out on paper. La Perra and her story lack any attribute that might have made her a novelistic character, even though she insists, believing herself to be nothing but a word, on being exactly that. She is not a character, but the expiation, through the forms given by the story, of a secret passion; ultimately, she will perhaps be the clarification of a mystery yearned for by the rest. A figure, nothing more, drawn against the night, which, like our own predicament, requires a monumental testimony to crucifixions, the penetration into an impossibility where her suspected reality dissolves once and for all or turns into words, still other words which, with their meaning, defend an unbridled knowledge of the passion invoked by her body and her eyes. Build her afterward as one would build a dyke, a great wall: by accumulation; grant her the

fate of subjugation, a flood. There's no doubt that the photograph was the representation of a premonition; something
like the as yet unclear scale of every attempt we have made
to confront the real fact that we are made manifest in the
convergence of every annihilation to which we could have
subjected her. The secret is this: she was chosen because she's
more vulnerable than the rest. In the crucial understanding
of this anguish, the imagined voice of the Pantokrator will
tell us the names of everything that makes up a definitive
sacrifice and the secret that those names hold. The meaning
will open itself up like her sex to the enlightening penetration of death. Perhaps that's what needs to be made clear in
the banal contents of the letter La Perra received and which
he read surreptitiously while she slept.

The people from the tent need actors to depict the Know-
it-all's metaphysical farces. They want to give a performance
tonight, just like we do. A chapter made up by X to fill
out the sketchy plot of *The Secret Crypt*. He had spoken at
length about this possibility. He called it the mental theater
and had worked out the basic principles of this dramaturgy.
'It deals with a visual annotation of these emotional gestures,' he told me, 'with the possibility of considering them
geometrically and linguistically thereby to obtain the primary graphemes of a strictly conceptual mime, which would
then allow the performance of certain dramatic gesticula-
tions.' X having said this, the Other found himself assailed
by a memory: a night of his life when a strange hand had
gesticulated so close to his eyes that it was impossible to
understand its language. Perhaps it was an amateur actor, of
course. Or the author suddenly called to the proscenium by

the audience. Or a drunken stagehand, who, in confusion, had suddenly interrupted the scene in the middle of the performance. Some embarrassing occurrence of this sort. It is therefore necessary to interrupt the drama, hastily to lower the curtain, to reassemble the stage, to shout for the lights: Lights! Lights! Lights! More light! To give the audience an explanation: We must beg your pardon for what just happened, and we hereby inform the audience that they can get a full refund at the box office if they so desire—an option that most will probably happily accept and act on immediately. That's why, when the book falls to her feet, as if she had heard it before, Mía says, 'In order for us to be real, it is necessary that he suffer, that he come down from his ivory tower and look us in the eye. He can imagine only what we think, not what we are, because he doesn't have the spiritual peace to distinguish between the two.' She remains pensive while going over her own appearances throughout the book. Too many disappearances. The readers will demand something else called genuine reality, with living, breathing men and women of flesh and bone. An insane imagining of Hell: men and women made of flesh and bone. The arguments responding to this objection are of an essentially technical nature, and are thus too tedious at this point. On the other hand, there is somebody who always keeps the desires of the reader in mind. The reader, like most women, feels a profound antipathy toward abstractions, or at least toward what their hatred of the simultaneous ideas of the reading defines as abstraction, and prefers to grapple with the mortal or sensitive qualities of the universe. In Mía's case, the reproach is a product of that essential quality of the statue that is its former presence, in the pages of this book, at the moment when Condillac conceives it as an idea.

'How can I explain to you,' says X, speaking of one of his novels, 'that what's important isn't that the characters be real, but that they be true.'

Sometimes, when we meet to speak beneath the tree, it seems like his mind abandons whatever giant conjecture he's always formulating and, although he speaks out loud, he's not really, addressing me.

'This book,' he says pensively, 'the book in which you and I are nothing but an image that you've perhaps imagined, is like a mirror and its nature is similar to the world. We are simply reflected in it. Every moment of which we're made is recorded in these pages and, for example, right now, it's not possible to read beyond this point, any further than here.'

'Here,' however, is an infinitely mobile here. The author of our book displaces 'here' as much as possible or as much he desires. The dream, the images between views are blurry moments that correspond to the intermediate points of that passage from here, the act of turning the page; that described moment when the woman has got to the end of a page and is about to turn it or let the book fall to her feet so that it opens, like she opens, to a passage determined by chance. 'Actually,' he continued, turning to me and staring, 'right now we form part of a scene where two men, you and I, talk about a book that we've imagined as something that has already been written and in which we assume ourselves to be contained. We are those vague presences that inhabit it, living something like a strictly literary tragedy.' He fell silent for a few moments and then turned his eyes aside.

'Now,' he adds, 'what might lead us to suppose that we are not the materialization of a madman's whim; a madman who believes himself a writer and claims to be the author of a book called *The Secret Crypt*, in which we, you and I, are nothing more than an image contained on page 106 Don't think that my words might have an ulterior motive, but whoever is in possession of the book already knows, so to speak, what will happen in the final pages. The aim of our organization was to deduce what happens after this or other pages, such as how the contour of a carved stone can hint at the entire design of the ruined cathedral of which it was once a part.'

Yes, it's about a skillfully hatched possibility, such as a crime.

X suspects that I am the author of the book and his suspicion manifests itself in the deliberate reading of another one of his little works of literary fiction.

'Listen to what I just wrote,' he says as he pulls a crumpled piece of paper out of his tunic. 'A novella. It's called *The Pyramids of Egypt*.' Then he begins to read:

'"Pseudo-T had begun to meditate on the principle employed by the architects who built the pyramids. Why are such constructions so perdurable? He sought advice on this problem from old E, the architect who loved to dream imaginary cities and who knew a few secret principles of construction.

'"'Tell me, why are these buildings eternal?'

'"And E replied:

'"'Because they were originally imagined after their collapse. The architects who built them had read ahead a few pages in the book in which they were characters. Those who didn't know that thought it was a holy book, until somebody realized that it wasn't a holy book, but a book that someone was writing.""

When he finished reading, he asked me, with a smile:

'What do you think? I'm sure,' he continued without waiting to hear my opinion, 'that you've also had that strange sensation, that feeling of being one of the characters in *The Secret Crypt*. I must confess that it happens to me often. Right now, for example. Can you imagine what it would mean for us if we had that book! Has it never occurred to you that one of us has already read it? La Perra maybe? You, for your part, always have ink-stained fingers and red eyes,' he said.

No, he didn't say that exactly. I didn't hear him clearly. The wind in the branches was too loud for me to hear the final words. Suspicion betrayed the suspect. I would have liked to ask La Perra if she already knew the contents of that book in which she and us, all the members of Urkreis, are apparently fictitious characters. But she wouldn't even have heard me because the Know-it-all had joined us on our walk. At the origin of all these things had been an image: a photograph in which Mía was surrounded by wreckage, leaning on an architectural vestige over what were clearly the grooves of an illegible inscription, etched into the stone; behind her, to her left, one could make out someone's hazy silhouette.

'This is not about that image by any means,' said the old man. 'It's about a different image, one that has nothing to do with that one. An image evoked by a remembered image.

Or the image that evokes an invented image. Or the image that evokes a lie and in which we are just the kernel of truth that all lies contain.'

Thus far, I thought, as the three of us walked toward the tent, we've barely begun to penetrate that anticipated world. We've longed for those tenuous epics recorded in a book that everyone has imagined, but which nobody, except maybe La Perra, has read. We've wanted to be the words composing a testimony that tells a totally fictitious story, one that never happened but which nevertheless is unquestionable, as is every shaky edifice constructed by the mind. Those tumescent environments in whose chinks we've thrived like poor, blind, immortal insects, awaiting an awakening to an absolutely perfect knowledge of our fate. We might set out thence, like pilgrims, in search of a red book. A pilgrimage that would have lasted fifty thousand years by the time we arrived at that stronghold, where whoever dreams us would wake up to show us a depraved model of the universe, built according to the description contained in *The Secret Crypt*, which is a book that contains the universe and which is also the description of itself; which is to say: a lie. It turns out, then, that this is nothing more than the legible man-ifestation of a total fallacy, due, it seems, to the fact that a detailed description of the clothing and psychological states of the characters has been left out of the text and the author has limited himself to describing the course of their thoughts and the realization of their ideas rather than their features. Or perhaps it's that we're not trying to obtain any specific knowledge of them?

'And all of this alludes to us?' La Perra asks me.

'No, it doesn't allude to us. It describes us fragmentarily. Or maybe fully. We don't know. We'll have to wait fifty thousand years to know, that is, if we really are as we've been described here. By then we'll have been a constantly repeating image for millennia.'

'And how did we look to them?' she asked.

'Like this, exactly like this, perhaps . . .'

My condition as a novelist is based on this response, and as such, I toil in pursuit of reality, an interior reality. The obsession drags me out of the never-ending flow of the Heraclitean river. My digressions: I wish they were worth something in life and not just in the novel. The characters in this book live as a function of the words that constitute them, of the fabrications that represent them. One might occasionally think that he is being written randomly, with neither pre-established plan of action nor passion. What happens is that there are an infinite number of Heraclitean rivers of reality. The initial outline, contained in a notebook that will get lost, has been substantially altered. The structure, inspired by *The Begum's Fortune*, isn't at all perceptible. The same axes along which the initial double plot unfolded: the contents of the anonymous letter that Mía received and the imaginary city conceived by E, now have but a diffuse presence in these pages, they haven't proliferated enough to become secondary accessories to the new plots emerging every moment as new possibilities. They're the little novels that X writes and which he recounts to me or lets me read in the shade of the tree where we meet to create this novel in which we are the characters, characters which, as the book progresses, become vaguer and vaguer, breathe each breath with more and more uncertainty, hidden behind the essential immateriality of the words they say, the words they write, or with which the Imagined writes them. There's an essence breathing in them that none of them have realized: they're nothing but poorly defined areas of reality, and what they were looking for was simply an instrument that would allow them adequately to re-enter it. That was the goal of the ceremony that someone, the Imagined or the Pantokrator, had organized.

We then headed for the tent. It would soon be night and we still didn't know whether La Perra would submit herself to the ritual. X met us before we arrived.

'Step right up, ladies and gentlemen!' The Know-it-all suddenly began to shout. 'Come see the dance of the sleep-walker who dreams the world! Come see the dance of the Fire Flower who embodies the mystery of the great solipsism, come!'

Guided by the Imagined's plan, we hurried down the dusty path, following La Perra, who walked in front, but whose gait, despite propelling her faster than ours did, was slower than ours—the old man's, X's, mine.

Now the Know-it-all calls the names of those who will participate in the ceremony. I go over to X and say into his ear:

'Who is that guy?'

But little did he seem to care about the identity of the Know-it-all. I suppose that X has, somehow, discovered a secret. I even think he knows what's on a subsequent page in the red album; that it was he who was lying in wait for the woman who, according to him, was reading us when we spoke in the shade of the tree; it was he who read the book, read a page beyond the present, when it slipped out of Mía's hands and fell to the floor, near where she met the man who was writing, and it was also he who surreptitiously read, while she slept, the anonymous letter she had received. That's why I think that we need to be on alert for other characters that we haven't even suspected. And of course, I'm absolutely free to think in these terms about my friend, now that his own imagination, as a forger of novels, will have imagined itself committing all these vile deeds. That would be why, instead of answering my question, he merely shrugged his shoulders and said, cavalierly:

'That doesn't matter anymore . . .'

A few steps farther he added, as if talking to himself:

'. . . What matters now is that we're about to receive news.'

We had gone twenty paces when all of a sudden, La Perra, who was ahead of us, came to an abrupt halt. We reached her stopping point unawares. We fell silent. La Perra seemed to be scrutinizing something on the crepuscular horizon. A few minutes later, we heard a murmur. A murmur like rats behind a wall, like glass shattering far away. It was a murmur subjected to the severity and gradual development of a process whereby that shapeless and distant rumor became a strange and rhythmic fact in the distance, something that was becoming known: a gallop.

At which point, a white horse appears in the book; a dot, barely visible on the horizon, which, in accordance with an absolutely inviolable law of arithmetical proportions, is growing larger as it approaches us. It is now a white horse galloping toward us over the plain. But before it arrives it veers and crosses in front of us at full gallop. We follow it with our eyes until it fades out of sight toward the ruins.

'That was foreseen, right?'

'Yes, on pages 12, 45 and on page 90.'

Somebody said these words. It's not actually out of the question that I pronounced those words, but it's also an irrefutable fact that, when we started to walk again, the Know-it-all turned toward X and said, ironically:

'Maybe tonight you'll deign to tell us about the consequences of the novel you're writing.'

We soon arrived at the tent, but night had already fallen.

'Come, gentlemen, come . . .' the Know-it-all said to us deliberately, as he planted himself next to the entry gate. 'Come hear the story of *The Secret Crypt* straight from the mouth of the author!' he shouted. 'Come learn of the adventures of the written-men! Step right up, ladies and gentlemen!' he kept saying, even after we had entered the moldy building, tremulously illuminated by decrepit footlights. The old dream that lay forgotten, across the months, across the years, across fifty millennia, suddenly re-awoke in my mind. 'Step right up, gentlemen, step right up . . . ! Come see the Mind That Is Suddenly Set in Motion . . . !'

The Know-it-all's words resonated with that intonation peculiar to certain passages of Italian opera and which always lends them a memorable character, despite their tenaciously banal and often even populist intent.

We sat on folding chairs in the second row, in front of a small platform adorned with a red velvet frieze seasoned and coated with a pattern of silver dust. The proscenium arch is decorated (. . . not with magic shapes, but . . .) with figures whose execution brings to mind the erotic scenes of Watteau and Fragonard, and in its center, it is crowned with an overelaborate medallion, the point at which the tattered hangings of the curtains part, also made of scarlet velvet and held aloft by a crude hook of rusty iron. There's an incomprehensible inscription etched on the medallion. It's possible that the hook is like the style of the gnomon, casting its shadow over the sundial of the medallion, which has a perfectly discernible, although illegible, inscription, whose message the Know-it-all pretends to know by means of what he calls the practice of the Fire Flower.

'Come, gentlemen . . . the ceremony that brings out memories!' The old man was still shouting from the tent door. 'A game of remembering forgotten things!'

I told you so.

Then he comes to join us.

'We don't have to get hung up on the details. We can't bore our distinguished audience with a tedious enumeration of the circumstances that have brought us here.' His tone sounds almost like a cheap advertisement. And he adds, 'This meeting was foreseen fifty thousand years ago. It is the moment when two things of equal value meet so that they can be exchanged, each being the most valuable thing that exists, but remaining worthless unless it is exchanged. Our situation, on the other hand, is urgent, as you will all understand . . .'

(Now he will show us an image.)

An image of a woman leaning on an architectural fragment appears on stage. Somebody has etched an inscription in the stone, illegible in the shadow (. . . like that cast by the style of the gnomon on the sundial . . .) that the woman casts over the stone.

'Who took that photograph? You're all wondering, aren't you?'

'(. . . La Perra . . .)'

'Who is the character that looms from behind, to the left of the woman, huh . . . ? While we prepare the next *tableau*, you can consider my proposition.'

Then, on stage, we see the scene where Mía is seen from the back, sitting near a window, reading a book with a red cover. Across from the window hangs a painting on which, at this exact moment, shines a beam of golden light, highlighting the beautiful coppery hues of the paint. It would seem to be a painting by Chardin.

What's going to happen now?' I ask X.

'It all depends on La Perra,' he quietly replies.

'And if he's the Pantokrator?'

'It doesn't matter. He needs to know the meaning of the inscription.'

The curtain closes. The Know-it-all stared at us for a while. He discerned our bewilderment.

'Yes,' he said, smiling, after a moment. 'It's possible that La Perra knows the meaning of that inscription; but I can't wake her up to ask. If I did, our world would disappear. This is obvious, right?'

'But then . . . the red book? Isn't the key to this mystery written in its pages?' I asked.

'Probably,' he answered immediately. He paused and then added, 'I'm sure the key to decipher this can be found in the book; but that book is still being written by someone, by you, or by the Imagined, as you call him, or by someone who, in any case, hasn't finished writing it yet, but who already knows our fate and, by writing it, can alter it . . .'

'But suppose,' I interrupted him, 'we know the contents of *The Secret Crypt*, then why assume that we've come here in search of the book?'

'Because I know that's not why you've come here,' he replied, smiling ironically.

X and I looked at each other in silence. The Know-it-all kept talking.

'. . . Your affiliation with Urkreis implies that you know the beginning of the book,' he said, 'but you don't know the end.'

''The end is always the present moment.'

'Only,' he said, his piercing stare boring into me, 'if we die in the present moment . . .'

'You sent the anonymous letter, which, according to the book . . .'

''That matters not at all,' he answered. 'Perhaps you haven't considered that this, too, was one of the little stories that X presumptuously calls his "novels"?'

'And what if it was?'

The Know-it-all stood up and began pacing back and forth, slowly, without looking at us. He kept his eyes fixed on the ground and seemed to be formulating a complicated idea.

'And what if it was,' I say after a while. 'Among ourselves, all of us can reconstruct the full contents of the book, along with a lot of other things.'

'And if this isn't the case?' asked X.

'Then we would have to wake La Perra that she might reveal her past and how it involves the photograph, that she might tell us the book's ending, the part we don't know. But if La Perra wakes up . . .'

Then the curtain drew back and we saw La Perra, who was asleep on a sofa. It was a reenactment of the moment the book falls from her hands to the floor, not of the stage, but of the auditorium, landing at the feet of the Know-it-all, who closed the curtain again and bent down to pick it up.

'Obviously,' he says sardonically as he puts it in his pocket, 'it's just a prop.'

He then turns to face us with a look simultaneously solicitous and decisive, his appearance is amplified in the flickering light of a few decrepit or misdirected footlights, which makes everything, every single glance, reveal his grotesque makeup, his essential mendacity, and then he says to us:

'. . . Or can anybody by chance presume that this,' he pointed to his pocket, 'isn't what you've come looking for? But we'll talk about that later.'

At which point, the curtain creeps open with a sober tranquility, like a geometrician about to demonstrate a formula.

'Watch this, for example . . . ,' he said.

'A washed-out photograph whose bilious yellow stains and iridescent edges contrast with the muted hues of gray and white, which an antique light, still present without the sun, developed on the sensitive emulsion of a photographic plate inside a large, vaulted building, with tall, wide walls over which the light was scattered in lambent patches.'

'It looks like the brightest part of a Vermeer, doesn't it? It's the first impression you get from the clash that individuality always brings about between two interlocutors as they employ a rather trite mode of communication. Upon closer inspection it reveals a figure that is, in many ways, reminiscent of one of those Spanish tombs with its reclining statues . . . But this, too, is a lie; a common lie induced by the memory of a Giuseppe Galli Bibiena architectural perspective, seen once, by chance . . . The space seems to transcend the limits of light, rising toward a brightness that eventually invades the darker images. You may have noticed this remarkable effect, of course,' he said, as the curtain that served as a backdrop closed once more. It was as if the vision of this image had lasted as long as a camera's shutter speed.

'What does the image mean? Is it an image from the book?'

'It might be from the missing notebook.'

'Which notebook?'

'The notebook that was lost and then reappeared here in the story . . .'

'Certainly,' says the Know-it-all, 'you absolutely must get it right . . . you are both judge and jury.' He looked condescendingly at the stage and added, in a tone that recalled the discussion about the geometrician, 'It's really a working photograph, hastily taken by a photographer more expeditious than expert, using a magnesium light and developed without properly stirring the chemical bath. After it was fixed, it wasn't dried correctly, as you can see by those yellow stains, which make it hard to discern with complete clarity what it depicts. Let us suppose that it is one of the pictures from the red book. What really matters—' here his words were more distinct '—is to know whether it's from before or after the current moment; whether it's an incidental or transitory image, an "example," say, for example, as is assumed about this little book,' he moved his hand to the pocket where he had put the book. Then he added, in an emotionless, informative tone, 'It's a photograph of a corpse. Our archive contains an infinite number of psychographic documents like this . . . some of them, like that one, do it in a downright brutal manner, but they all express our disturbing relationship with death. The photograph of Gavrilo Princip, for instance . . .' The red velvet curtain was drawn to reveal a face on the stage. '. . . That picture comes from the photograph of a passion, not from the portrait of an exceptional assassination. You shouldn't assume that this makes me somehow complicit with the *komitadjis*. I'm simply illustrating the possibilities of another language, taking an example from the journalistic iconography of our own times . . .'

'Can you show us more pictures like these?'

The image lingered for a few moments before the Know-it-all turned to conceal the stage.

'I can show you as many as I like, but only you can specify whether these images were taken before the current moment, though you won't know if they will be taken in the future or the transitory present since you're unaware of which page of the text you're on . . .'

'You're alluding to that same old identification between writing and life.'

Before continuing, the Know-it-all turned and sat on one of the folding chairs in the front row, with his back

to us. He let out a cavalier, almost sarcastic, sigh, and said
resignedly, as the lights in the tent, but not on stage, gently
went dark:

'I often think that our author has it in for us when he
puts such endlessly redundant words in our mouths, such as
what the text calls the "identification between writing and
life." What else could be expected from our condition as
creatures that, really, just come to life, in some vague way,
in the present moment, that is, if we are being written, in
the interior gaze that guides the hand holding the pen?'

'What happened to the deleted chapters?'

'Ah!' he exclaimed, 'the chapter about the deleted chapters is perhaps the most interesting of all!'

'They might be images that we show ourselves; just translated into a strictly visual language.'

'Indeed. After the earlier stages, choosing the discipline
allows the projection of a self-seeing image for the initiate;
that is, an image that reflects whoever looks at it, somehow,
bearing witness to themselves.'

The projected image depicts a scene where a woman and
a robe-shrouded priest meet in a deserted park. It's winter.
They sit on a bench. The woman takes out a cigarette and
the man offers her a light from a golden lighter. The woman
speaks and the cleric listens. The woman shows him a letter,
which she takes out of her handbag. The cleric doesn't finish
reading it. He folds it with contempt and returns it to the
woman. He looks around suspiciously and, with gestures
that denote a habitually authoritarian manner reluctantly
suppressed, speaks for a few moments. But we can't hear
what he says. The image disappears.

We feel as if a secret fact has been revealed to us.

'That's an image of the past, right? It might also be an image of the future, or a suppressed image, past or future, isn't that right?'

We don't know how to respond. Nobody says anything.

'It's a suppressed image of the past,' he says. And then adds, 'Through the experience, he tried to escape the plan that radiates toward us from the pages of the book.'

How can we incorporate the entire plan and become characters of the true version that the author suppressed, cast recklessly into the trash and then reread by a spy or a stranger, many years later; not many years later, but actually only a few; many enough for the pages—written in the paroxysm of some turbulent excitement that almost always ends up sidetracking the course of the story—to acquire stains as if from tea spilled on their edges and the words that inhabit them like insects lose all meaning? Might it be that the truth of the world, the truth we aspire to learn, resides in the trash cans of insane asylums, the terminus of our worldly knowledge?

We are silent for a few moments. X whispers to me that this was, as the Know-it-all had already informed us at the beginning of the performance, a game of remembering forgotten things, and nothing more. The Know-it-all, who had surely understood X's gossip, his hypothesis about our true nature, and disapproved of it, suddenly says:

'Experience advises me to distrust those who assume that they are pieces in a complicated game without being able to admit an unflattering consequence of such a state of affairs: that they might be the loser's piece.'

'It's blatantly obvious that you're interested in dragging us into a game, which, besides already being an unoriginal literary conceit . . .'

'It's not that,' interjected the Know-it-all, 'it's not that at all.' He took a breath, 'We don't have much time. The Zentrum's agents will soon be here; they were sent subsequent to the subversion of Urkreis. By any means necessary, they'll try to shut down this experience that we have embarked on, without our really realizing it until this moment. If we're able to escape and pool our resources, we'll have established a new core group that will give us absolute control of the Zentrum . . .'

'What about the others? E, H the geometrician, pseudo-T, her . . . ,' says X pointing vaguely in the direction of the stage.

The Know-it-all continued talking, impassive.

'Pseudo-T is dead. You can make several conjectures about that sad fact. Pseudo-T might have taken his own life for personal or private reasons that don't concern you. In which case he will have written the decryption over the blurry rubbing of the inscription you had given him to translate. When you went to pick up the translation, there was a premature indiscretion in the text, which was later crossed out or amended; pseudo-T noticed the true plans lurking beneath the surface of the investigation and refused to return the rubbing upon which he had, inadvertently, recorded the key to *The Secret Crypt* in his own handwriting. So then you turned to the last resort and managed to recover the rubbing and acquire a fact, the knowledge of which makes it possible to obtain very advantageous results . . .'

'Another hypothesis would be that perhaps it was you who did away with pseudo-T, for fear of being denounced for your excessive interest in a question whose importance the victim had yet to realize when the inscription was decoded, and which pseudo-T had yet to tell anyone about.'

'These are possibilities,' said the Know-it-all, 'as are many other scenarios that we can't dwell on, such as, for example, that perhaps pseudo-T was done in by agents of Polt, in order to suppress, among other things, the looming possibility of the inscription being translated since it is secretly thanks to this possibility, foreseen by the old members of Urkreis, that this indolent and drunken character was admitted into the organization in the first place, although not even he knew that. Regarding H and the architect, it's better to assume that they were crossed out, like two smudges necessary to the inner harmony of a tenaciously revised and perfected drawing.'

'What about her?'

'La Perra? She is the drawing.'

Then he made the giant tree in the middle of the plain appear. Two men meet, deep in conversation. Now we can hear what they're saying. One of them says: 'Then they are led by a mysterious man to a chamber that contains the universe . . .'

'You see,' says the Know-it-all. 'I am that mysterious man.'

'You can bring us there?'

'That's where we have to hide.'

'Let's go then. There's no time to lose.'

'When we arrive you'll hand over the inscription that pseudo-T decoded.'

'Okay. Let's go.'

The Know-it-all leads them down a dark passageway behind the stage. They proceed with difficulty as La Perra has trouble walking through the darkness. They follow her a few steps farther as she wanders through a dream from which nobody would dare to wake her, because it's not yet the right time to do so. The heat rises perceptibly as they go deeper into that narrow, resonant corridor. They stop suddenly. The Know-it-all turns toward La Perra, takes her hand, and says:

'Are you ready to go farther? Are you ready to consummate the experience?'

La Perra nods her head and they continue walking into the darkness.

Their flight leads them, imperceptibly, into the domain of the Imagined. As they advance through the somber passageway they sense the intimate relationship they're establishing with one another, willing as they are to suffer together through the demands of the experience thrust upon them in their obsession with being characters in an adventure novel originally conceived along the more or less simplistic lines of *The Begum's Fortune*. They make their way toward a space where time no longer passes. That's what the Know-it-all has told them. A static image of the world that was the goal of the ceremony they intended, the background of their own dreams, where they would be able to see themselves in the mirror before somebody opened the floodgates that would release a fate suppressed by highly complex thought processes, which would spill forth, over the world, subsequently causing its annihilation. As they moved forward, nothing enabled them to envision the end of the march. Occasionally, running their hands over the textured walls of the tombs that line the passageway, they find symbols engraved by someone else. Their fingertips trace the outline of glyphs that express nothing but the silence that envelops all, the desperation which, just as silently, preys on them. A desperation so subdued that it prevents them from giving up, but quite the opposite, incessantly pushes them onward, as if at the end of the suffocating tunnel they sensed a magnificent expanse of light, of space. But that's not true. The darkness, furrowed only by our footsteps, by our fatigued breath, is the sole, vague, painful indication of our presence there, among the shadows.

What more do we need to do in order to develop this novel that somebody is writing about us? Keep walking down this dark passageway, run our blind hands over the symbols that others before us have inscribed, fifty thousand years ago. Inscriptions that tell of long voyages, falls, crossings with no point of departure and no destination.

Although it might be assumed that the vast length of this tunnel had been excavated in a straight line, the Know-it-all has informed us that it's a very wide curve, which, as it progresses, creates a peculiar space blessed with unique properties.

'The end of the tomb is reached via a space that appears to be some form of narrow opening, but which is actually a sort of double torus composed of an infinite number of Möbius strips; it leads everywhere in the world while simultaneously closing in on itself, and, in reality, it doesn't lead anywhere at all.'

At some point along that space lies the chasm that contains us from outside of itself, and in which our path is represented as something contained in a receptacle, which, in turn, is contained in what it contains; contained within the pages of a book, a book that someone left at some unknown point of that distinct, continuous surface.

'There are mirrors here,' said the Know-it-all, 'mirrors in which it's possible to see the Other reflected in the silence that almost never takes part in the conversation.'

The atmosphere becomes more and more oppressive. Unforeseen forces begin to intervene, as we advance, in our interpretation of reality. We are very far from, yet very close to, everything. We keep walking. Now it seems like we're slowly marching, like soldiers overwhelmed by a distant or inner drumroll. Pulsations. Seventy per minute.

'Those awkward voices that narrate us with increasing vagueness . . .' says La Perra as she covers her ears with her hands.

'Maybe we've arrived back at the point from whence we set out.'

'It's possible, but then we would be others. We would already be those the Imagined is writing. Clearly defined words, homonyms.'

We stop to rest. La Perra continues to stand, leaning against the wall which, with its subtle curvature, delimits the space contained in the plane across which we proceed.

'We've penetrated the interior of a machine,' says our guide, 'a metageometrical machine.'

'How can you guarantee that we're not dead?' asks La Perra.

'That's an apt hypothesis, given the circumstances, but entirely improbable,' answered the Know-it-all.

In their total lack of clarity, the characters in *The Secret Crypt* accept the demonstrative types of data that science provides about its condition within the Möbius passageway. They don't yet realize that the author of the book which contains them combines those data according to his own absurd whims; they don't notice that, even though they're now part of one order, they're being narrated within another.

They set out again. They soon become prey to despondency. The continuity of everything within the order wherein they are now inscribed as figures—as shadows wandering erratically along a secret, sinister corridor—is on the verge of insanity. Leaning against the walls in the dark, they try to find the meaning of this adventure. Suddenly they hear a weak shout, barely audible, but infinitely persistent, a shout that echoes cyclically through the interminable, fraught cavity that continues forever into itself.

It is La Perra who screams.

'Look!' she exclaims. 'A shadow . . . there.' She points in an unexpected direction, where our eyes, drowning in blackness, slowly discover a hazy silhouette.

'Stop!' shouts the shadow. 'Don't move, or I'll shoot.'

Then it illuminates them with a flickering light, moving toward them. Its features can't be distinguished behind the light.

'Who are you?' it asks. 'What are you looking for here?'

La Perra is scared. She grabs me, groping blindly, imperceptibly; she takes my hand without anyone else realizing it.

The shadow reaches us, revealing itself in the glare of the light pouring from it.

'It's H, the geometrician,' says La Perra.

H points a pistol at us, glowering at each of us menacingly.

'I should have guessed. It's you guys . . . ,' he says.

'You decided to act on your own. Are you coming or going?'

'It doesn't matter,' he says, putting away the pistol and taking a drag on a cigarette, which, in the higher vibration of the light, momentarily sets the contours of our gloomy mood ablaze. He continues in an indifferent tone, without looking at us.

'I see that you decided to act on your own, too. At this point there's nothing left to betray.'

'Did you find the stronghold?'

'Hmm . . . maybe,' he smiled sadly. 'Maybe I found what I was looking for . . . Or maybe I too am dead, without being totally sure about it.'

He shot us a final contemptuous look and walked off in the other direction, smoking. He hadn't gone ten steps when he stopped and turned, calling to us.

'Perhaps you guys will be more useful than I was,' he said, tossing the pistol, which landed at my feet as he started walking again. We heard the cadence of his footsteps retreat until every trace of him was gone. The only remnant of his presence was a barely demonstrable memory. I put the pistol in my pocket.

'Let's go,' said the Know-it-all. 'The geometrician is dead and we've wasted a lot of time.'

We started walking. Our footsteps tediously echoed against
the walls. From time to time we could hear the Know-it-all's
voice amid the panting breath that wheezed from his tired
chest as if his speech were made of poorly linked fragments.

'He wasn't prepared to enter this place,' he said, referring
to H. 'He didn't know about the existence of the book in
which his death was perhaps already recorded. Coming all
the way here availed him nothing . . . An impetuous man
who didn't know how to take advantage of his formulas
and principles . . . if he's not dead already, he won't get out
of here alive.'

Every so often he issued a few words, as if thereby he
might alleviate his fatigue, lighten the load that weighed
heavy on his mind.

'Anyway,' he said, pointing to La Perra, 'her presence
safeguards us from any setback . . . We're not breaking any
of the rules of the game . . . We have a right to visit this
region's museums . . . Don't we . . . ? Well then . . . ? Don't
fall behind . . . We have to get to the stronghold before the
agents from Polt reach the ruins.'

The atmosphere was growing more and more oppressive.
We were having difficulty breathing, and our only prospect,
aside from suddenly arriving at the same point where we
entered the passageway—a geometrically impossible circum-
stance if H really had died or if we were not going to find
him again, this time catching up with him from behind—
would be to retrace the path which, in the case of that tunnel whose peculiar form the Know-it-all defined as '. . . a
double torus composed of an infinite number of Möbius
strips . . . ,' would always take us in the direction of a single

point along it: the point at which we would have wanted to retrace the path; an action which we could no longer take, or so it seemed, until we reached the stronghold where it would be possible to obtain the information we had come in search of, which would allow us to return once the agents sent by Polt abandoned their plan to wipe us off the face of the earth, if not from its bowels.

We walked a long while until we reached a point where the passageway was barred by a small door radiating a quadrangle of yellowish light. The Know-it-all opened it and we entered a sparsely furnished room. A sensation of memory and relief emanated from the small chamber. The walls were an ochre color. Behind some chintz curtains, frayed at the edges, could be seen the white frame of a window. In a corner, a man slept on a bunk. Mía went to wake him.

'It's F., the architect,' she says.

'Leave him alone!' The Know-it-all says in an irritated tone. 'He's dreaming cities. When he wakes up he'll tell us what he's seen.'

We settle in for a rest.

'Have we fallen into a trap?'

'Are there pacts between the members of Urkreis and the members of the Zentrum that we don't know about?'

'What matters now,' says the Know-it-all, 'is that we've left the continuity of the tunnel. Perhaps we've cleared the first stage. We have to stick exclusively to the evidence. H is dead. So much is certain. Otherwise he would be here . . .'

'And us? Are we dead?'

'I don't know . . . It doesn't matter . . . It really doesn't matter at all.'

E, who had woken up and was stretching, rubbed his eyes and said:

'Of course it doesn't really matter at all!' We all turned towards him. 'It really doesn't matter!' he said again and yawned, spreading his arms as if crucified. 'Well . . . ,' he then said, sitting up, 'to what do I owe the pleasure of this unexpected visit?'

He rose from the bunk, half-asleep, shaky, and came over to the small table where we were seated. He sat down and, leaning on his elbow, stared at each of us in turn.

'Such bafflement behind that indifference!' he said.

He poured himself a glass of water and took a sip.

'Ah . . . !' he exclaimed with satisfaction, as if the strength that had apparently abandoned him during his dream had now returned. 'Or is it that you've come to eliminate me on behalf of the others . . . ? Huh . . . ?'

We made no reply. E's face became sad and he lowered his eyes.

'But how?' he said ironically.

'Are you dead?' asked Mía.

'You've crossed the geometrical corridor and you don't know its properties! Ambushed! *Freischutzen*! How could you belong to a *Camerata*, whose only purpose was the study of geometry! Scum, colluding with the shady fraud of the litho-ptikon! That's what you were! Vain words spoken in secret or in the shade of a giant tree in the middle of a plain, right?'

'It's not true! You're mistaken.'

Ah, E has gone crazy! Or so the false geometricians would have said on finding themselves discovered, on find-ing themselves unmasked before the inescapable gaze of the Know-it-all, who would have seemed indifferent to not only the words, but also the presence of E if it hadn't been for that frigid stare, as if it were the fixed center of the world, focused on a bit of cigarette ash that had landed on the tablecloth, near Mía's left hand, illuminating, so to speak, a subtle consideration of the number of combinatorial possibilities that the writing suggested at that moment. Among those combinations—where time is nothing more than a system of order in the space of the board on which white and black pieces are themselves the space that they occupy—what most clearly comes to mind is the combination that informed the possibility that the members of Urkreis wanted to keep secret the sheet of paper with the rubbing and translation of the sundial's epigraph, and that everyone else was in collusion with E.

But the truth was something else.

'H!' E exclaimed melancholically. It seemed that he had already revived his dream: H the geometrician had literally turned into the *demonstratio* of his *propositio*! E smiled.

"The condition of H the geometrician is a subject on which we can't spend too long,' said the Know-it-all. 'There's not much time left . . .'

'Actually, that can be overlooked here,' interjected E.

But after a brief pause the Know-it-all carried on, impassive.

'. . . And we've come all the way here to carry out an operation that allows us to proceed or go back . . .'

'Here, both journeys are of a nature different than that which we ascribed to them back there,' E interjected again, pointing his index finger at the room's soffit.

'It doesn't matter,' continued the Know-it-all, 'we've adopted different methods. That's all. Now we need your help to proceed. In return, we'll take you with us on our way back. First we have to get to the stronghold.'

'Ah! The stronghold . . .' said E sarcastically.

'You have to tell us about it, understand?'

'I don't know anything about it . . .' said the architect, but then his eyes came alive and he added, almost without a break, '. . . except for one thing.'

'What thing?'

E stood up and, as he made his way to the other side of the room, said:

'Something you obviously don't know yet.'

When he reached the chintz curtain he turned toward us.

'Come here,' he said, calling us with a gesture of his hand.

We followed him. E turned his back on us and brusquely drew the curtain. The light from the room, reflected on the glass, prevented us from seeing through the window, which E then opened wide onto the darkness.

'Look . . .' he said.

It was a vast nocturnal panorama. A suffocating sky, reddish almost to the point of blackness, like an enormous fold in a velvet cloth, a radiant city, as luminous as scattered jewels, near a sea that narrowed on the horizon, becoming a river whose source was always in the exact center of the view.

'You didn't believe me, did you?' he said, as in bewilderment we contemplated this incredibly vast landscape, whose fundamental property, which we had all grasped by now, was that of being contained; as if those distant, marvelous cities rising from below had sprung forth or emerged from the water at whose edge they rested—from the depth of the ocean toward a space that was, again, wholly interior.

Each of us questioned him with our eyes.

'I'm dreaming it,' said E after a few minutes.

'Is that where the stronghold is?' asked the Know-it-all.

'Perhaps,' he replied, 'but I can't see beyond my dream.'

'What does that mean?'

'That I can't see beyond what can be seen,' he said, 'that the images you're looking for aren't part of my dream.'

'Who lives in those cities?' asked La Perra.

'Us . . . Nobody . . .' he replied.

'How do we get there?' asked X without taking his eyes off the view through the window.

"That's up to you. It's impossible for me to lead you any farther. I haven't been able to go any farther than this myself. It's impossible for me to break out of this dream.'

'Can we?'

'We're going to try,' said the Know-it-all, 'but first we have to seal the deal.'

'We can't give you the rubbing until we've made it past this insanity,' said X as he turned toward E, who, upon hearing these words, merely gave a contemptuous shrug of his shoulders.

The Know-it-all withdrew from the window and began to pace around the room, pensive.

'It's not as easy as you think,' he said. 'Once we penetrate that panorama, we'll turn into someone else's dream; into the dream of someone who's not dreaming what we see beyond the window, which is E's dream, but what is really there,

what actually exists there. It would require some mechanism
that would allow us to escape his will or his awakening.'

Then he stopped, as if he had found a solution.

'. . . We could immortalize his dream,' he continued,
addressing E. 'Isn't that an expression you yourself have used
to define . . . that . . . ?' he said, pointing in the direction of
the window. 'We could kill you, for example . . .' He kept
pacing. 'We could kill you once we're certain that the panorama you've shown us, which you say is your dream, won't
disappear as soon as you die. Instead, it will be immortal-
ized or will become everlasting with your disappearance,
because it's your dream.' He stopped again and reflected
on this. 'But how to carry out two operations at the same
time?' He continued pacing. 'How to kill you from inside
a dream that you're dreaming?'

We all remained silent. E didn't seem very worried about
the fate that the Know-it-all had in store for him.

'I'll stay here to watch him,' said X.

'Yes,' agreed the Know-it-all. 'It would be advisable for
us to split up until we arrive at the edge of the next phase,
where we can await the arrival of whoever stayed to watch E.
But when we get there, X will have to eliminate you, since
we can't run the risk that you'll forget us once we've gained
access to the stronghold . . .'

'But then how will we get back if all that, the city, disappears with his death?' asked X.

'The city will no longer be his dream; it will be our memory, through which you'll be able to find us. This place
would become part of the story that contains us, it would
be indelible, so to speak; we could take it anywhere, at our

leisure, without the fear that you might abandon us.' Then
he spoke to E. 'Without the fear that you'll make us disappear from your dream. You could also denounce us to our
pursuers; that is, if they get here." Then the Know-it-all
became grave and said, as if talking to himself, 'Yes, it's better for X to stay here until we've crossed to the next phase.'
Then he turned to me. 'Give him the pistol.'

I gave it to him. X cocked the gun as he headed for the
windowsill on which E leaned, indifferent, his back turned
to us. When X reached his side and pointed the gun at his
temple, E didn't bat an eyelid.

'Let's go,' the Know-it-all went on, 'there's no time to
waste. It's essential that E doesn't become demoralized or
stop dreaming his dream, of which we'll be a part.'

We jumped out of the window and became invisible as
soon as our feet touched the ground; we looked at the view
one last time before setting forth. A darkness lighter, but
also more troubling, amplified the sound of our footsteps
and fully submerged us in its blackness. We only saw them
briefly, at long intervals, those will-o'-the-wisps that bore
faraway witness to the immeasurable distance, to the mysterious and endless space that we—La Perra, the Know-it-all,
and I—had now entered. Nevertheless, a strange sensation
weighed on us, like the sensation of being enclosed in that
vast space, as if in a coffin. We walked a few steps. La Perra
turned back around, trying to find the window to E's room,
but in vain: Turn around; slowly . . . drink in the faint,
intoxicating light that seeps through the windowpane. But
now, forget, forget everything . . . twist around yourself like
a reptile . . . don't say anything . . . maybe you don't even

exist . . . you're just a word spoken in the darkness, a hazy
character in a story, perhaps a meaningless story, where the
premonition and obliteration of everything that happens is
methodically recorded.

That's how I invoke her as we walk; drifting away from
I don't know where.

We continue in silence. We're now guided by a plan dic-
tated to us by the Imagined. The landscape we saw from E's
window forms a reality that leads us on a long walk through
memory to the vicinity of an enormous tree shaking its
outstretched branches over a featureless plain. The wind
brings us voices. The murmur of a conversation lost in the
remotest depths of memory. As we move nearer, the voices
disperse, and by the time we arrive to take shelter and rest
against the tree trunk, the participants in that ambiguous
conversation have disappeared.

'It is foreseen that you give me the rubbing here,' the
Know-it-all says to me.

'X has it,' I reply. 'We have to wait until he gets here.'

We wait in silence. After a little while, beyond the murmur of foliage shivering in the wind, the characters notice
the sound of weary footsteps. A presence lurking near the
tree. It's pseudo-T. When this apparition becomes clearer,
La Perra's face floods with furious terror.

'You're dead,' she says, her voice trembling.

'No, my condition is more horrific than that,' says the
new arrival.

'Bah!" exclaims the Know-it-all, barely looking at him.
'If you had stayed there, in the ruins, you'd be deader than
you are now.'

'That's what you would have wanted, right?' said pseudo-T as he sat down beneath the tree. He added pensively,
'Yes, something definitely more horrific!'

'Like what?'

'Like being wrong.'

'Wrong? Did you manage to reach the stronghold?'

'If I had managed to reach the stronghold, I wouldn't
have been wrong.'

'What do you mean by that?' the Know-it-all demanded
in a startled voice.

Pseudo-T was silent for a few moments while his eyes
tried to find, in the shadows, or as if looking for music in
the noise of the foliage swaying above our heads, the gaze
and attention of the Know-it-all. Finally he said:

"The decryption of the rubbing is wrong. There's an
error . . .'

The Know-it-all didn't say a word. His mind formulated
strange conjectures about the possibility that pseudo-T was
trying to scare him away and that the decryption was correct after all.

'You haven't been able to get past this tree?'

'Space stops beyond the shadow of this tree. Actually,
that is space: the shadow cast by the tree.'

'Nonsense. Metaphysical speculation. Banalities. You're
a stupid drunk old fool.'

It may be a flawed translation of the inscription that
appears in the photograph, but the old scoundrel's metaphysical speculations weren't entirely misguided. It was necessary, then, to wait for X. He would have to say something
now, under the foliage of that enormous tree. Perhaps he

would tell us about some ridiculous adventure in which we would be the characters. We would secretly demand a good prophecy from him. We would demand a novel in which the characters sufficiently fulfill the fate that the author imposes on them.

No. Enough. The pause has become sketchy, as if the Imagined were hesitating, as if the pen between his fingers had seized up. The spectators demand significant facts. They're free to go to the ticket box and collect a full refund if what's happening has ceased to interest them. They shout demands that the hidden pages of the book be read. They demand that the meaning of the inscription be revealed. Ah, the forever fruitless wait that books are made of! Other panoramas, more distant, more visible than the one that terrifies us now. We're on the threshold of an emotional crystallization of our contiguous presences, Perra. I look at her reclining against the tree trunk, hidden behind her dream. X has arrived undetected. Her words now ring out, while I watch her sleep, as if they were the words of another story. A distant narration. A distant light in itself, but capable of revealing to us the face of this dementia, of this dream. The structure of this immense cavity holding us in its mystery is being built before our eyes. A titanic prison where thought wanders around in chains, held like a small sphere in the lifeless fist of a corpse.

'You mustn't implement the catechumens until consciousness has been demolished like a vile statue . . .'

It's X's voice. We cried out for absolute oblivion. Listen, Perra: everything is circumstantial now, as the Know-it-all would have said. Circumstances. Vain circumstances that the mind summons to crush us. But you'll have to wake up. I'll snatch you away from the dream in which you are dreaming us, in front of the definitive image of that other character who, at the solitude of his desk, resolves his virtual life by writing the incidents of a yet to be reported conspiracy against time on the pages of an album bound in red Moroccan leather. Look: the darkness has opened up around us. We're clinging to marmoreal tombs. Structures foreseen after their decomposition everywhere surround us. Ah! What calm, what silence emanates from these cracks! Don't speak. Don't say anything. The symbiotic moment will only happen in front of the mirror.

'The Other, the one who hitherto has only heard the story is slowly waking to the state where his passion for La Perra has a clearer meaning. This is how he comes up with the idea of dropping everyone else . . .' X recounts into the night.

Shadows that the storyteller casts into the night. Perhaps that's a phrase that appears in the book, and with which the awkward novelist, who invents everything, perhaps tries to save himself from his own gaze. A gaze that might blind him. Surely he remembers—since, like the Know-it-all, he's fond of classical engravings from the classical period—those etchings which, in their spontaneous and subtle graphics, depict a density of shadows so shaded that the light near them is darkened; he remembers how the artist's prints depict prisons, universes composed of bleak materials and corroded by a dim light like vitriol dissolved in spring water. Maybe it's the world that exists behind the little forums that Galli Bibiena designed to be so well lit and which seem to emanate a luminosity that impregnates everything around them, defining everything with such precision—as with the light that accentuated the infinite limits of the bodies there represented—that they open up those majestic perspectives. How can a gaze contain so much space without falling apart? Without straying toward those devious spatial conformations that allow the symbiosis to be fulfilled by use of the senses alone? But that's a thought on which we cannot dwell, especially if we consider that we don't have much time. The audience that so gallantly showed up for the spell of the dance of the Flower of La Perra, dancer-hypnotist, will lose patience and the spectators will start asking for a refund, and despite the fact that you, sir, are an honest businessman, you are also an improvident businessman for having squandered every possibility of providing satisfaction to the fucking masses, fired up with impatience and beginning to shout: 'What happened?! Come out, you sons of bitches! Start the show! Send La Perra of Fire out! Send the sleepwalking priestess out!' They demand compensation for the fact that you don't have the translation of the inscription that appears in the photograph of La Perra. An inscription that you, sir—without understanding its meaning in the slightest, despite knowing how enormously important its meaning is—have represented in the medallion that crowns the decorations made by some popular artist over the proscenium arch and which are reminiscent of the style of Watteau or Fragonard and have nothing that suggests the mysterious symbols that adorn the façades of alchemical books. The inscription that appears—as if engraved on the concave surface of a spherical dial whose perspective is skillfully created through its own parallels and meridians, which design the whole composition and determine an already different hyperspace that contains or is contained by the dial over which the gnomon casts a shadow marking an hour once a year, and which corresponds to the hour when the sun's rays are projected on the dial at such an angle that the outlines of the characters composing the inscription darken just enough that, if seen from an angle similar to that of the camera lens at a height more or less equal to the average height of the eyes of a man on the ground, that is, from a position similar to that of the photographer who captured the plaque—the inscription that appears to shape, through a plot hatched by someone who has combined a subtle, almost demonic, knowledge of cosmography, descriptive geometry, and chiaroscuro, his solution of logical continuity in the form of a message that serves as a model, throughout fifty millennia, says X, or would say, so that the members of a secret tradition locate the book that contains them as characters and subsequently know their own fate and that of each and every person.

Throughout the millennia of their search, they have established enormous subterranean archives where, by means of a binary classification system, they store the fate of men in an infinite number of directories—fat volumes printed on ordinary paper with cardboard covers. Those volumes are just encoded catalogs of small, private libraries, modest collections of curious books, in some of which, in the worn-out and re-read copies, we are written, in the past and future, as a succession of words. In this photograph, the shadow cast by the sun over the sundial would have

given us an excellent indication of the hour it was taken,
were it not for Mía, who appears to the side and in front
of the block with the sgraffito-engraved sundial and who
casts her own shadow over it, which indicates the direction
the sun is shining and its angle during periods that include,
we may theoretically assume, precise time lapses of certain
lengths, and taking into account that the quarry stone with
the sundial can be pointed, by design of the dial, in only two
directions: west and east, and also taking into account the
inclination of the ecliptic, the inclination of the vertical axis
of the Earth, as well as the annual position of all this over
the elliptical orbit around the Sun, and furthermore, the fact
that Mía is dressed appropriately for fall, the contrast of the
photographic density that has already been studied according to the sensitivity of the emulsion in different longitudes
and latitudes and according to altitude or temperature, and
the film being sensitive enough to reveal, to within an hour,
the time when it was exposed; the look of the vegetation
and the aggregation of dust, by defined foci, in the area
around the bases of the monuments which give an exact
enough indication of the direction of the predominant
winds and the intensity with which they erode the edges
of blocks scattered by other cataclysms across the whole
plain that extends to the horizon behind Mía and which, if
these were of a geologic nature, could easily be traced with
data contributed by other circumstances and thus revealed.
But these investigations have been disrupted by suspicion,
by the secret initiative and ambition of the others, so it
has been important to act promptly, every man for himself, bringing about the formulation of sub-cells inside the

original cells, composed of the secret membership of every new group that has established itself and carried out the same operation that the Pantokrator carried out in the heart of his organization until he created the Zentrum after his self-exclusion from every other organization, but the other way around; through the affiliation of all the super-secret groups, generally formed by couples of men and women whose affinity is expressed in the overt nature of that continuity with which the secret tradition of writing a book in linked letters persists throughout the history of the species.

"Did you hear that? A shot. Don't be alarmed. That means that we'll get to the stronghold soon, because X just killed the Know-it-all there, in the distance, under the crown of that immense tree. Fear not. It was foreseen. It was necessary. Come. Take my hand. I'll guide you. You're very tired. The journey has been exhausting, I know. Don't falter; we're so close to the stronghold. We'll be there in a second. We'll go into the passageway like this, hand in hand. X dreams us entering that huge compound that contains the other space to which you aspire, right? A space different than that other one. A space that contains everything and is contained in everything. Look, everything around is like a mirror; the substance that inspires this scene is the reflective. Everything is forever reproduced. It's a construction that's inhabited in an alveolar arrangement. The chrysalis of something grows in each alveolus; a minor entelechy, in the vocative, of what is here this instant and what has there yet to be. It is, for us, a museum of styles. Everything here, the outline of friezes recorded by a Michelangelesque hand, the grand analytic machines with their woodwork scaffolding captured in cyclopean knots of convoluted cordage. Alphabetical knots that express a hidden, but banal, meaning; the strange effects of light visible in the interior of a few alveoli that have been devised by perceptive stagehands. A sinister coldness emanates from other gaps, as if the essences of things that have been and will not recur for another fifty thousand years are breathing therein, do you understand? You and I are in alveolus em-one-two-seven-three; here it is, come . . . Everything is also like a book, successively, to infinity, because the alveoli are monumental passageways that, from one side to the other, open onto deceptive little cubicles, conceived according to the principles by which Borromini designed the false perspective of the Palazzo Spada. The characters of this book live in those cubicles," says X, letting out a guffaw that rises, resonating sinisterly between the branches of the tree swaying in the wind; but my own guffaw is inward. Inside that cubicle the collections are contained, protected from the dust in glass cabinets and *cappelle* with green or black marble foundations, along with little bronze plaques that have designations etched in English, such as *The Anonymous Letter, The Uttered Man, The Pyramids of Egypt, The Red Book* . . . Beyond that, the Chinese, do you see them? They're the ones who guard the doors that lead to the sea, a sea of rats eager to devour the universe. The image is very clear right now, despite the amplification and carelessness with which the plaque was revealed, without stirring the hyposulphite bath. The lithoptikon is contained in that glass cabinet, a trick of the mind.

It's a small cube of basalt, bored through in the shape of a vesicle. That's where the paleontological specimens are: the piece of amber with the mayfly . . . We have to get here.

It's a Here that is constantly shifting.

'Stop,' he says. 'Don't go too far, no more than a few steps. Go toward the interior of the cubicle if you can. Look, stand there. Lie on the sofa next to the lucarne. Yes, like that . . . with your back to me . . . Ah, you can get a memorable image out of these details! Wait. Don't move. Calm is essential to induce the symbiosis. We're about to enter into a pure relationship with the Imagined, who is writing us. Don't get distracted. On the wall opposite you there's a painting that's about to receive, full on, a golden beam of light that penetrates through the oval window. It's not possible to distinguish the contents of the painting because the depiction appears to be almost on its side. Your hair is a scribble of shadows, like embers on the verge of burning out. There's a red book next to you. It's possible that it's an analogical copy. Don't open it yet. Can you hear me clearly? The instructions I'm giving you? We're going to continue, then. Rest your elbow on the back of the sofa. The sofa is a peculiar piece of furniture. The lateral volutes of the curved back are made by a woodcarver proficient in the teachings of the Brotherhood. In between them you can see a unicorn's head. Now set your other hand on the book by your side. Like that. Very good. When I tell you, take the book, open it, and start reading, but not before I tell you. You have to wait until the light hits the painting exactly. At six twenty-three P.M. Almost there.

'Now. Start reading the book.

'Tell me; tell me what the book says . . . What? A horse? A few men and a woman who see a white horse gallop over the seashore? Ah! For a moment I thought you were confused, that you had taken one character for another, but that's not true, is it? What happened is that this is a prop copy. No doubt about it. That's not where you have to read, but further on. Skip a few pages and read me a little . . . What did you say? A woman receives a letter, yes . . . about a secret organization called Urkreis. No, that's before. Skip a few more pages . . . The drawing? No, no! What's happening is that you're on the other side of the mirror and the pages there follow one another in reverse—do you understand? You have to read toward the other side. (Trans-temporal alveoli . . .) The photograph of a corpse on a dissection table . . .That could be before or after. Skip a few more pages, but in the other direction . . . That's it! Of course! That's you and I, yes, naked. You open yourself to me like the door to a deserted house. But we want to know what happens further on, when he and she have already entered the stronghold . . . Who is Herminester Ille Exhumatus? The Pantokrator? No, of course not, how stupid! A little Chinese box . . . Yes, which contains the world . . . Where is it? It's important. Do you hear me? You have to tell me where the box is. Pay attention. Read with extreme care. Pay close attention . . . And the rats? You have to find out what happens with the rats . . . Who is the Fire Flower . . . ? Yes, of course. You are the Fire Flower.'

Then La Perra reads herself. That image is contained in the book. It's as if she had devoured herself or as if she were the amphisbaena that simultaneously slithers in two opposite directions. It's a mysterious passing toward a depth below words. Toward the depth where they aren't yet separated from the substance that makes them meaningful as written representations of a reality that is totally alien to them.

Close the book when you reach the end of the page and sit up to face the alveolar passageway, outside of the cubicle represented by October 13. She couldn't sleep that night, and to while away the forced hours of wakefulness imposed by her insomnia she drew a picture in pencil on a sheet of notebook paper, using her fingertip to blend and shade. That drawing, whose reflection we've just seen in the mirror, bears witness to the veracity of these declarations since therein she clutches in her fist her insomnia and the date it occurred. Ever since that night, the events that surround us have been occurring. We're free, however, to interpret the continuity of those events in whichever manner best suits our interests. We're free to assume that it's an image glimpsed through a door that is ajar, opening onto a room in the Pensione Pistoj, in Fiesole. Mía was tired. That morning they had walked to the Roman theater. On the way back they decided to take a shortcut through the vineyards but ended up taking a break in the hemp fields surrounding the cemetery, until they found the highway again, where they joined the owner of the guesthouse, whom they had befriended and who was walking back to Florence right then with a package of books under his arm. Second-hand books, which, once read, became part of the boarding house's small public bookcase, situated in the first-floor lounge. From the window on the left side you get a splendid view of the city crossed by the Arno, with the cupola, the Campanile del Duomo and the Torre di Palazzo Vecchio in the distance, in the valley. Images of sculptures from the recently visited Cappella persist in her memory. Surely you remember that walk. I'm sure you remember that walk we took during an imaginary trip. The owner of the guesthouse was named Herr Prahler, or something like that, right?

The telephone is ringing.

"There's the Imagined! Did you see him? Get ready. Now we've arrived . . . Yes, that's it . . . There he is! Shush! Don't make any noise. He's writing in reverse. Let him keep writing . . . When I tell you . . . Here, look. Yes . . . The hand holding the pen hesitated, the words he just wrote provoked the feeling that someone was lurking behind him.

One voice, as if it had already been heard fifty millennia ago, resonates in his memory of voices and seems to say: . . . Let him keep writing . . . When I tell you . . .

The suppliant voice of someone giving instructions to a ritualistic killer in an uncertain ceremony . . .

'Now!'"

MICHAL AJVAZ, *The Golden Age.*
The Other City.

PIERRE ALBERT-BIROT, *Grabinoulor.*

YUZ ALESHKOVSKY, *Kangaroo.*

FELIPE ALFAU, *Chromos.*
Locos.

JOE AMATO, *Samuel Taylor's Last Night.*

IVAN ÂNGELO, *The Celebration.*
The Tower of Glass.

ANTÓNIO LOBO ANTUNES, *Knowledge of Hell.*
The Splendor of Portugal.

ALAIN ARIAS-MISSON, *Theatre of Incest.*

JOHN ASHBERY & JAMES SCHUYLER, *A Nest of Ninnies.*

ROBERT ASHLEY, *Perfect Lives.*

GABRIELA AVIGUR-ROTEM, *Heatwave and Crazy Birds.*

DJUNA BARNES, *Ladies Almanack.*
Ryder.

JOHN BARTH, *Letters.*
Sabbatical.

DONALD BARTHELME, *The King.*
Paradise.

SVETISLAV BASARA, *Chinese Letter.*

MIQUEL BAUÇÀ, *The Siege in the Room.*

RENÉ BELLETTO, *Dying.*

MAREK BIEŃCZYK, *Transparency.*

ANDREI BITOV, *Pushkin House.*

ANDREJ BLATNIK, *You Do Understand.*
Law of Desire.

LOUIS PAUL BOON, *Chapel Road.*
My Little War.
Summer in Termuren.

ROGER BOYLAN, *Killoyle.*

IGNÁCIO DE LOYOLA BRANDÃO, *Anonymous Celebrity.*
Zero.

BONNIE BREMSER, *Troia: Mexican Memoirs.*

CHRISTINE BROOKE-ROSE, *Amalgamemnon.*

BRIGID BROPHY, *In Transit.*
The Prancing Novelist.

GERALD L. BRUNS, *Modern Poetry and the Idea of Language.*

GABRIELLE BURTON, *Heartbreak Hotel.*

MICHEL BUTOR, *Degrees.*
Mobile.

G. CABRERA INFANTE, *Infante's Inferno.*
Three Trapped Tigers.

JULIETA CAMPOS, *The Fear of Losing Eurydice.*

ANNE CARSON, *Eros the Bittersweet.*

ORLY CASTEL-BLOOM, *Dolly City.*

LOUIS-FERDINAND CÉLINE, *North.*
Conversations with Professor Y.
London Bridge.

MARIE CHAIX, *The Laurels of Lake Constance.*

HUGO CHARTERIS, *The Tide Is Right.*

ERIC CHEVILLARD, *Demolishing Nisard.*
The Author and Me.

MARC CHOLODENKO, *Mordechai Schamz.*

JOSHUA COHEN, *Witz.*

EMILY HOLMES COLEMAN, *The Shutter of Snow.*

ERIC CHEVILLARD, *The Author and Me.*

ROBERT COOVER, *A Night at the Movies.*

STANLEY CRAWFORD, *Log of the S.S. The Mrs Unguentine.*
Some Instructions to My Wife.

RENÉ CREVEL, *Putting My Foot in It.*

RALPH CUSACK, *Cadenza.*

NICHOLAS DELBANCO, *Sherbrookes.*
The Count of Concord.

NIGEL DENNIS, *Cards of Identity.*

PETER DIMOCK, *A Short Rhetoric for Leaving the Family.*

ARIEL DORFMAN, *Konfidenz.*

COLEMAN DOWELL, *Island People.*
Too Much Flesh and Jabez.

ARKADII DRAGOMOSHCHENKO, *Dust.*

RIKKI DUCORNET, *Phosphor in Dreamland.*
The Complete Butcher's Tales.

RIKKI DUCORNET (cont.), *The Jade Cabinet.*
The Fountains of Neptune.

WILLIAM EASTLAKE, *The Bamboo Bed.*
Castle Keep.
Lyric of the Circle Heart.

JEAN ECHENOZ, *Chopin's Move.*

STANLEY ELKIN, *A Bad Man.*
Criers and Kibitzers, Kibitzers and Criers.
The Dick Gibson Show.
The Franchiser.
The Living End.
Mrs. Ted Bliss.

FRANÇOIS EMMANUEL, *Invitation to a Voyage.*

PAUL EMOND, *The Dance of a Sham.*

SALVADOR ESPRIU, *Ariadne in the Grotesque Labyrinth.*

LESLIE A. FIEDLER, *Love and Death in the American Novel.*

JUAN FILLOY, *Op Oloop.*

ANDY FITCH, *Pop Poetics.*

GUSTAVE FLAUBERT, *Bouvard and Pécuchet.*

KASS FLEISHER, *Talking out of School.*

JON FOSSE, *Aliss at the Fire.*
Melancholy.

FORD MADOX FORD, *The March of Literature.*

MAX FRISCH, *I'm Not Stiller.*
Man in the Holocene.

CARLOS FUENTES, *Christopher Unborn.*
Distant Relations.
Terra Nostra.
Where the Air Is Clear.

TAKEHIKO FUKUNAGA, *Flowers of Grass.*

WILLIAM GADDIS, JR., *The Recognitions.*

JANICE GALLOWAY, *Foreign Parts.*
The Trick Is to Keep Breathing.

WILLIAM H. GASS, *Life Sentences.*
The Tunnel.
The World Within the Word.
Willie Masters' Lonesome Wife.

GÉRARD GAVARRY, *Hoppla! 1 2 3.*

ETIENNE GILSON, *The Arts of the Beautiful.*
Forms and Substances in the Arts.

C. S. GISCOMBE, *Giscome Road.*
Here.

DOUGLAS GLOVER, *Bad News of the Heart.*

WITOLD GOMBROWICZ, *A Kind of Testament.*

PAULO EMÍLIO SALES GOMES, *P's Three Women.*

GEORGI GOSPODINOV, *Natural Novel.*

JUAN GOYTISOLO, *Count Julian.*
Juan the Landless.
Makbara.
Marks of Identity.

HENRY GREEN, *Blindness.*
Concluding.
Doting.
Nothing.

JACK GREEN, *Fire the Bastards!*

JIŘÍ GRUŠA, *The Questionnaire.*

MELA HARTWIG, *Am I a Redundant Human Being?*

JOHN HAWKES, *The Passion Artist.*
Whistlejacket.

ELIZABETH HEIGHWAY, ED., *Contemporary Georgian Fiction.*

AIDAN HIGGINS, *Balcony of Europe.*
Blind Man's Bluff.
Bornholm Night-Ferry.
Langrishe, Go Down.
Scenes from a Receding Past.

KEIZO HINO, *Isle of Dreams.*

KAZUSHI HOSAKA, *Plainsong.*

ALDOUS HUXLEY, *Antic Hay.*
Point Counter Point.
Those Barren Leaves.
Time Must Have a Stop.

NAOYUKI II, *The Shadow of a Blue Cat.*

DRAGO JANČAR, *The Tree with No Name.*

MIKHEIL JAVAKHISHVILI, *Kvachi.*

GERT JONKE, *The Distant Sound.*
Homage to Czerny.
The System of Vienna.

JACQUES JOUET, *Mountain R.*
Savage.
Upstaged.
MIEKO KANAI, *The Word Book.*
YORAM KANIUK, *Life on Sandpaper.*
ZURAB KARUMIDZE, *Dagny.*
JOHN KELLY, *From Out of the City.*
HUGH KENNER, *Flaubert, Joyce and Beckett: The Stoic Comedians.*
Joyce's Voices.
DANILO KIŠ, *The Attic.*
The Lute and the Scars.
Psalm 44.
A Tomb for Boris Davidovich.
ANITA KONKKA, *A Fool's Paradise.*
GEORGE KONRÁD, *The City Builder.*
TADEUSZ KONWICKI, *A Minor Apocalypse.*
The Polish Complex.
ANNA KORDZAIA-SAMADASHVILI, *Me, Margarita.*
MENIS KOUMANDAREAS, *Koula.*
ELAINE KRAF, *The Princess of 72nd Street.*
JIM KRUSOE, *Iceland.*
AYSE KULIN, *Farewell: A Mansion in Occupied Istanbul.*
EMILIO LASCANO TEGUI, *On Elegance While Sleeping.*
ERIC LAURRENT, *Do Not Touch.*
VIOLETTE LEDUC, *La Bâtarde.*
EDOUARD LEVÉ, *Autoportrait.*
Newspaper.
Suicide.
Works.
MARIO LEVI, *Istanbul Was a Fairy Tale.*
DEBORAH LEVY, *Billy and Girl.*
JOSÉ LEZAMA LIMA, *Paradiso.*
ROSA LIKSOM, *Dark Paradise.*
OSMAN LINS, *Avalovara.*
The Queen of the Prisons of Greece.
FLORIAN LIPUŠ, *The Errors of Young Tjaž.*
GORDON LISH, *Peru.*
ALF MACLOCHLAINN, *Out of Focus.*
Past Habitual.

The Corpus in the Library.
RON LOEWINSOHN, *Magnetic Field(s).*
YURI LOTMAN, *Non-Memoirs.*
D. KEITH MANO, *Take Five.*
MINA LOY, *Stories and Essays of Mina Loy.*
MICHELINE AHARONIAN MARCOM, *A Brief History of Yes.*
The Mirror in the Well.
BEN MARCUS, *The Age of Wire and String.*
WALLACE MARKFIELD, *Teitlebaum's Window.*
DAVID MARKSON, *Reader's Block.*
Wittgenstein's Mistress.
CAROLE MASO, *AVA.*
HISAKI MATSUURA, *Triangle.*
LADISLAV MATEJKA & KRYSTYNA POMORSKA, EDS., *Readings in Russian Poetics: Formalist & Structuralist Views.*
HARRY MATHEWS, *Cigarettes.*
The Conversions.
The Human Country.
The Journalist.
My Life in CIA.
Singular Pleasures.
The Sinking of the Odradek.
Stadium.
Tlooth.
HISAKI MATSUURA, *Triangle.*
DONAL MCLAUGHLIN, *beheading the virgin mary, and other stories.*
JOSEPH MCELROY, *Night Soul and Other Stories.*
ABDELWAHAB MEDDEB, *Talismano.*
GERHARD MEIER, *Isle of the Dead.*
HERMAN MELVILLE, *The Confidence-Man.*
AMANDA MICHALOPOULOU, *I'd Like.*
STEVEN MILLHAUSER, *The Barnum Museum.*
In the Penny Arcade.
RALPH J. MILLS, JR., *Essays on Poetry.*
MOMUS, *The Book of Jokes.*
CHRISTINE MONTALBETTI, *The Origin of Man.*
Western.

NICHOLAS MOSLEY, *Accident.*
Assassins.
Catastrophe Practice.
A Garden of Trees.
Hopeful Monsters.
Imago Bird.
Inventing God.
Look at the Dark.
Metamorphosis.
Natalie Natalia.
Serpent.

WARREN MOTTE, *Fables of the Novel:*
French Fiction since 1990.
Fiction Now: The French Novel in the
21st Century.
Mirror Gazing.
Oulipo: A Primer of Potential Literature.

GERALD MURNANE, *Barley Patch.*
Inland.

YVES NAVARRE, *Our Share of Time.*
Sweet Tooth.

DOROTHY NELSON, *In Night's City.*
Tar and Feathers.

ESHKOL NEVO, *Homesick.*

WILFRIDO D. NOLLEDO, *But for*
the Lovers.

BORIS A. NOVAK, *The Master of*
Insomnia.

FLANN O'BRIEN, *At Swim-Two-Birds.*
The Best of Myles.
The Dalkey Archive.
The Hard Life.
The Poor Mouth.
The Third Policeman.

CLAUDE OLLIER, *The Mise-en-Scène.*
Wert and the Life Without End.

PATRIK OUŘEDNÍK, *Europeana.*
The Opportune Moment, 1855.

BORIS PAHOR, *Necropolis.*

FERNANDO DEL PASO, *News from*
the Empire.
Palinuro of Mexico.

ROBERT PINGET, *The Inquisitory.*
Mahu or The Material.
Trio.

MANUEL PUIG, *Betrayed by Rita*
Hayworth.

The Buenos Aires Affair.
Heartbreak Tango.

RAYMOND QUENEAU, *The Last Days.*
Odile.
Pierrot Mon Ami.
Saint Glinglin.

ANN QUIN, *Berg.*
Passages.
Three.
Tripticks.

ISHMAEL REED, *The Free-Lance*
Pallbearers.
The Last Days of Louisiana Red.
Ishmael Reed: The Plays.
Juice!
The Terrible Threes.
The Terrible Twos.
Yellow Back Radio Broke-Down.

JASIA REICHARDT, *15 Journeys Warsaw*
to London.

JOÃO UBALDO RIBEIRO, *House of the*
Fortunate Buddhas.

JEAN RICARDOU, *Place Names.*

RAINER MARIA RILKE,
The Notebooks of Malte Laurids Brigge.

JULIÁN RÍOS, *The House of Ulysses.*
Larva: A Midsummer Night's Babel.
Poundemonium.

ALAIN ROBBE-GRILLET, *Project for a*
Revolution in New York.
A Sentimental Novel.

AUGUSTO ROA BASTOS, *I the Supreme.*

DANIËL ROBBERECHTS, *Arriving in*
Avignon.

JEAN ROLIN, *The Explosion of the*
Radiator Hose.

OLIVIER ROLIN, *Hotel Crystal.*

ALIX CLEO ROUBAUD, *Alix's Journal.*

JACQUES ROUBAUD, *The Form of*
a City Changes Faster, Alas, Than the
Human Heart.
The Great Fire of London.
Hortense in Exile.
Hortense Is Abducted.
Mathematics: The Plurality of Worlds of
Lewis.
Some Thing Black.

RAYMOND ROUSSEL, *Impressions of Africa.*

VEDRANA RUDAN, *Night.*

PABLO M. RUIZ, *Four Cold Chapters on the Possibility of Literature.*

GERMAN SADULAEV, *The Maya Pill.*

TOMAŽ ŠALAMUN, *Soy Realidad.*

LYDIE SALVAYRE, *The Company of Ghosts.*
The Lecture.
The Power of Flies.

LUIS RAFAEL SÁNCHEZ, *Macho Camacho's Beat.*

SEVERO SARDUY, *Cobra & Maitreya.*

NATHALIE SARRAUTE, *Do You Hear Them?*
Martereau.
The Planetarium.

STIG SÆTERBAKKEN, *Siamese.*
Self-Control.
Through the Night.

ARNO SCHMIDT, *Collected Novellas.*
Collected Stories.
Nobodaddy's Children.
Two Novels.

ASAF SCHURR, *Motti.*

GAIL SCOTT, *My Paris.*

DAMION SEARLS, *What We Were Doing and Where We Were Going.*

JUNE AKERS SEESE,
Is This What Other Women Feel Too?

BERNARD SHARE, *Inish.*
Transit.

VIKTOR SHKLOVSKY, *Bowstring.*
Literature and Cinematography.
Theory of Prose.
Third Factory.
Zoo, or Letters Not about Love.

PIERRE SINIAC, *The Collaborators.*

KJERSTI A. SKOMSVOLD,
The Faster I Walk, the Smaller I Am.

JOSEF ŠKVORECKÝ, *The Engineer of Human Souls.*

GILBERT SORRENTINO, *Aberration of Starlight.*
Blue Pastoral.
Crystal Vision.

Imaginative Qualities of Actual Things.
Mulligan Stew. Red the Fiend.
Steelwork.
Under the Shadow.

MARKO SOSIČ, *Ballerina, Ballerina.*

ANDRZEJ STASIUK, *Dukla.*
Fado.

GERTRUDE STEIN, *The Making of Americans.*
A Novel of Thank You.

LARS SVENDSEN, *A Philosophy of Evil.*

PIOTR SZEWC, *Annihilation.*

GONÇALO M. TAVARES, *A Man: Klaus Klump.*
Jerusalem.
Learning to Pray in the Age of Technique.

LUCIAN DAN TEODOROVICI,
Our Circus Presents . . .

NIKANOR TERATOLOGEN, *Assisted Living.*

STEFAN THEMERSON, *Hobson's Island.*
The Mystery of the Sardine.
Tom Harris.

TAEKO TOMIOKA, *Building Waves.*

JOHN TOOMEY, *Sleepwalker.*

DUMITRU TSEPENEAG, *Hotel Europa.*
The Necessary Marriage.
Pigeon Post.
Vain Art of the Fugue.

ESTHER TUSQUETS, *Stranded.*

DUBRAVKA UGRESIC, *Lend Me Your Character.*
Thank You for Not Reading.

TOR ULVEN, *Replacement.*

MATI UNT, *Brecht at Night.*
Diary of a Blood Donor.
Things in the Night.

ÁLVARO URIBE & OLIVIA SEARS, EDS.,
Best of Contemporary Mexican Fiction.

ELOY URROZ, *Friction.*
The Obstacles.

LUISA VALENZUELA, *Dark Desires and the Others.*
He Who Searches.

PAUL VERHAEGHEN, *Omega Minor.*

BORIS VIAN, *Heartsnatcher.*

LLORENÇ VILLALONGA, *The Dolls' Room*.

TOOMAS VINT, *An Unending Landscape*.

ORNELA VORPSI, *The Country Where No One Ever Dies*.

AUSTRYN WAINHOUSE, *Hedyphagetica*.

CURTIS WHITE, *America's Magic Mountain*.
The Idea of Home.
Memories of My Father Watching TV.
Requiem.

DIANE WILLIAMS,
Excitability: Selected Stories.
Romancer Erector.

DOUGLAS WOOLF, *Wall to Wall*.
Ya! & John-Juan.

JAY WRIGHT, *Polynomials and Pollen*.
The Presentable Art of Reading Absence.

PHILIP WYLIE, *Generation of Vipers*.

MARGUERITE YOUNG, *Angel in the Forest*.
Miss MacIntosh, My Darling.

REYOUNG, *Unbabbling*.

VLADO ŽABOT, *The Succubus*.

ZORAN ŽIVKOVIĆ , *Hidden Camera*.

LOUIS ZUKOFSKY, *Collected Fiction*.

VITOMIL ZUPAN, *Minuet for Guitar*.

SCOTT ZWIREN, *God Head*.

AND MORE . . .

CPSIA information can be obtained
at www.ICGtesting.com
Printed in the USA
JSHW061054010822
28697JS00003B/5